INTERF

INTERFERENCE

TERRY GRIMWOOD

Elsewhen Press

Interference
First published in Great Britain by Elsewhen Press, 2022
An imprint of Alnpete Limited

Elsewhen Press, PO Box 757, Dartford, Kent DA2 7TQ
www.elsewhen.press

British Library Cataloguing in Publication Data.
A catalogue record for this book is available from the British Library.

ISBN 978-1-911409-86-1 Print edition
ISBN 978-1-911409-96-0 eBook edition

Designed and formatted by Elsewhen Press

This one is for Holly with love from Grandalf

He wept and at that moment, Torstein Danielson was no longer Secretary for Interplanetary Affairs. He was a grieving father. It was not the first time he had cried over his daughter since he left Earth, but it would have to be the last. He was alone in his quarters, onboard the *Kissinger*. The starship was two days out of its quantum tunnel and a handful of hours from its destination. He had work to do.

Driven to his knees, Tor let the sobs choke themselves out. There was no use fighting it. The breakdown would have happened sooner or later. Better now. Better to grind the truth into himself and force out as much of the grief as he could before the real business of the voyage began.

Was this his fault? Was this divine retribution, poured down upon him because of his adultery? If so, why punish his entire family? Eva was only sixteen, for Christ's sake. Why not strike the sinner down with a coronary or an assassin's bullet and leave his loved ones alone?

He allowed his mind to replay the personal com-link that was the cause of his emotional collapse. Over and over it went, every detail a lethal blade that sliced open his heart and made him bleed.

The link was with his wife, Annika. Her holo-image had been remarkably intact, despite the distance, especially the icy coldness of her grey eyes. Annika Danielson had stayed with him after the affair ended. She believed, she had said at the end of the long desolate night that followed Tor's confession of adultery, in the vows made at their wedding. Yet the wound Tor had inflicted on their marriage was deep and he wondered if it would ever heal.

When Annika spoke, her voice was quiet, clear and unemotional. "Physician Ang says that the cancer isn't responding to the latest treatment. The tumour is too deep within Eva's brain for it to be operable, even with nano-surgery." She paused. Then added; "The Priest is on standby. If you want to say goodbye to our daughter, you have to come home before it's too late. If you don't…

1

well, to hell with you." The link was cut. The holo-image dissolved in a sparkling waterfall of twinkling pixels. He could not go home to Earth, of course. Annika knew that. Firstly, he was too far away. Secondly, this mission outweighed all personal concerns.

The door comm beeped then opened before he could call out an invitation.

It was Lisa Kavanagh, Press Officer and guard-wolf.

"They're ready for you, sir."

*

Here was another hard thing to face; Katherina Molale, member of the embedded journo-pack. She was here at Tor's personal request, seated in the front row. The hurt at seeing her for the first time since their affair ended was more of a shock than Tor had anticipated. Nevertheless, he needed to maintain his composure. This was politics.

He scanned the rest of the pack, assembled here in one of the ship's smaller conference rooms. They were the inevitable mix of familiar and unfamiliar, the benign and the hostile, old friends, old foes and potential new enemies.

There was a moment, punctuated by the usual human sounds; coughs, throat-clearing, a whispered exchange. Then near silence, undercut by the gentle roar of the ship as it closed on Ia at incomprehensible speed. Tor cleared his throat but it didn't clear the hoarseness from his voice when he spoke.

*

Katherina was startled by the strain etched into Tor's normally inscrutable features. He looked tired and distracted. His discomfort was evident even before he took his place at the table between his twin minders. On his right, that poisonous elf Lisa Kavanagh. On his left, his Chief Advisor Shu Qingchun who blinked nervously behind his fashionably vintage spectacles (fashionable among the intelligentsia that is, apparently the cumbersome antiques were supposed to endue an air of wisdom on the wearer).

Tor's poorly concealed distress was almost a relief. A cruel one, perhaps, but the sight of his hurt diverted her focus from the brutal emotional wrench of seeing him again. In the flesh. Real. Here. She could guess why he looked so ravaged. His daughter. Bad news, no doubt.

Tor looked as if he was trying to hide behind the battery of comm-mikes and holovid-cameras arranged on the table's leading edge. Worrying, because Tor was normally the consummate media dancer.

Lisa, on the other hand, was hawk-like and aggressive. She scanned the audience as if daring anyone to ask a question she deemed awkward and promising fiery vengeance on any who did. This mob of sycophants were, Katherina decided, hand-picked and embedded by Lisa as the least troublesome. So why am *I* here? she wondered. Because she was no sycophant and she was most definitely troublesome, particularly to Torstein Danielson.

"Thank you for coming," Tor said at last. "Please be kind to me, as I know you will be." His affable smile was as forced as the assembled journos' laughter.

Katherina was up before anyone else had even moved. She was glad to note that her marine-trained reflexes were still sharp. "Mr Secretary, can you confirm or deny the rumours that the Alliance is prepared to offer military assistance to the Iaens?"

Tor's smile shifted towards genuine. "Good evening Ms Molale. I can deny them, categorically. I am here on a fact-finding mission, on behalf of Earth and Earth alone. Although a member of the Alliance of Planets, in this instance we do not represent them. The Iaens have made their request to Earth only. I intend to find out what assistance we can render during this crisis. As you know, I hold the deciding vote in the Earth Assembly –"

"That would be the vote on whether Earth should directly interfere in the Iaens' war."

"Please be assured that I will not vote until I am sure of the facts."

"So, to be clear, Mr Secretary, the Alliance have no part in these negotiations?"

"None whatsoever. They will not interfere in the affairs of any member planet unless they deem it to be a threat to the Alliance itself."

"But Earth will."

"Earth is, as you well know Katherina –" First name? Slip or deliberate? Whichever it was, it gave her a small, and unexpected, shock of delight. "– a signatory to the Interplanetary Alliance's Non-Interference Treaty."

"But surely even talking to the Iaens about the crisis *is* interfering."

"It is at their request and, as you also know, they are a founder member of the Alliance."

"Is it true that all six of the other Earth Assembly Chief Secretaries have voted for military aid to the Iaens, despite the Alliance injunction on direct interference, and that there is mounting pressure for you to do likewise?"

Lisa struck. "Ms Molale –"

"Mr Secretary, there is a detachment of marines on this ship –"

Lisa tried again. "I think you've had your turn Ms Molale –"

"– at company strength, if my calculations are correct. That doesn't feel like diplomacy to me."

"Hardly an invasion force."

"But boots on the ground nonetheless Mr Secretary."

"We are entering a war zone. Surely it makes sense to protect ourselves," Tor said. Katherina could tell that he thought the answer as weak as she did. He even offered what she took to be an unnervingly apologetic smile.

"Do the Iaens' enemy possess space-capability?" Katherina asked. "We haven't been told much about them." She managed a cynical chuckle. "In fact, we haven't been told anything at all." God, it was painful being hostile to the man she still loved.

"Information gathering about the conflict and its cause

is part of my brief."

"But would we give military –"

"I really think we should allow someone else to speak," Lisa snapped. "We don't have much time."

"It's alright, let her finish the question," Tor said.

Lisa glanced at him, clearly annoyed at being overridden, even by her beloved boss.

Katherina seized her opportunity. "Can you confirm that Earth is not going to offer direct military intervention in this conflict."

"If the Iaens request some form of assistance then we are prepared, in consultation with the Alliance, to provide them with a defensive, and I repeat *defensive*, protection zone. This would be space-originated. No marines will set foot on Ia's surface other than as ceremonial escort and security when our delegation planet-falls this evening."

"A historic event by the way," Shu put in, his smile suitably grave. "We are the first humans ever to be invited onto Ia itself."

"Is that a firm promise," Katherina pressed on. "That, apart from your honour guard, no marines will be deployed on the surface?"

"As firm as it is possible to make it," Tor said.

"That seems ambiguous –"

"Another question please." This time Lisa won. Despite her frustration, Katherina felt she had done well enough. That last vague affirmation of Tor's was a tightly stretched tripwire and from the look on his face, he realised it as well.

*

"Sir?"

"Yes, Lisa."

"We've had the usual requests for one-to-one interviews."

"I love an optimist. Planet-Fall is in an hour." Tor, already wearing his lander suit sighed and held out his hand for Lisa's noter. She passed it to him. He scrolled down the list. Then stopped.

"Katherina Molale. I'll speak to her."

"Are you serious? There isn't time and –"

"I'll give her ten minutes."

"I still don't understand why she's embedded with us."

"We need her scepticism and hostility. She sees through the fog, Lisa."

She knew. Everyone knew, but few ever mentioned the truth about Katherina Molale and Torstein Danielson.

Lisa put her hand on his arm. "Please," she said quietly. "Be careful."

"I will."

A moment then the door opened to admit Katherina and suddenly they were alone together. The first time since…Tor tried not to think about that. For some reason, her presence wrenched at his grief for his dying daughter. He managed to regain control and indicated, brusquely, towards one of the cabin's chairs. "Sit, please. Would you like a drink?"

"No, thank you. I need my stomach empty for planet-fall." Katherina sat down and studied him carefully. "Why am I in the pack, Tor?"

Her neglect of the correct form of address unnerved him, but he let it pass. He needed Katherina to be comfortable and he needed her to feel able to approach him and communicate.

"You're here to add a little spice to the general sycophantic blandness."

"Is that the only reason?" She sounded uncharacteristically ill-at-ease.

"Of course not. You are one of the best journos I know. *That's* why I need you. I want you to dig deep and I want you to cause trouble. The truth is in short supply around here, and it's going to be even rarer down there on Ia."

"It's good to know where I stand." Was that an edge in her voice? Anger, hurt even? There was an awkward silence, then she smiled. "Sorry. This is…difficult."

"For me, too."

"What do you mean by the truth is rare down on Ia? Do you think the Iaens are lying?"

"Why do they need *our* help? They are practically gods compared to us."

"A test?"

"Possibly."

"What do *you* think, Tor?"

"I'm keeping an open mind."

"Do you believe in this mission?"

"What? Of course –"

"The truth, Tor. I won't necessarily print it, but I need it if I'm going to be your spy."

"My spy? No –"

"What am I then?"

Tor sighed. "My spy."

"What do I get, in return? Earth gets its hands on more Iaen toys, you get the glory and a step closer to the presidency. What about me?"

She held his gaze and at that moment Tor wanted nothing other than to kiss her. He wanted *those* times back.

"How about a Pulitzer?" He felt his good humour and warmth drain into bleakness. "You're welcome to all the glory you want, none of it holds much appeal for me at the moment."

"I'm sorry," Katherina said, "about Eva."

"It doesn't matter what I do, I can't save her…"

His self-control shattered. This time he was not alone. This time Katherina was there and she held him and it was good.

*

Planetfall in a lander was a return to the primitive; solid fuel rockets, weightlessness, then atmospheric entry with all the horrors that entailed. Before it began, however, Tor, was treated to a full beauty-shot of the *Kissinger*.

Earth's new generation of Iaen-technology starships never ceased to take his breath.

The *Kissinger* resembled a huge spoked-wheel. Its cargo of humans and all their accoutrements were housed in the vessel's gleaming rim. The hub of the wheel was a plain sphere, which contained a minute sliver of white-dwarf matter, the source of the ship's internal gravity.

The quantum drive was external to the ship, a shimmering, multi-coloured orb of energy that encased the entire vessel in a bubble of light when hurtling it between the stars. Though dormant for the final, conventional, ion-driven sprint to Ia, the drive's translucent veil was still a thing of beauty. When engaged, the drive was brighter than Earth's sun. Like most sane people, Tor did not fully understand how the drive worked. He knew that it was fuelled by dark energy and its operating principles were down to the incomprehensible fact that, according to quantum physics, objects could be in multiple places at the same moment.

General anaesthetic was mandatory for both passengers and crew when the quantum drive was energised. There was no choice. It was sleep or insanity.

"Okay, final run-through," Tor said as much to distract himself from what he knew was coming as for preparation for his meeting with the Iaens. He was addressing his advisors who, like himself, were strapped into their seats and already looking pale and nauseated.

Shu uttered his habitual nervous cough. "The Iaens are the first extra-terrestrial race encountered by Earth, when they came to the aid of the colony seeder *Star Queen* twenty-seven years ago. They gave us the principles of light-plus travel and were invaluable in helping humankind establish links and relationships with other races in the Interplanetary Alliance. Little is known of their culture, etiquette or social organisation. In verbal interaction, they are blunt and direct, but this could be an effect of our translators."

"Can you state categorically that we are the first humans to be allowed access to their planet?" Tor said.

"Bit late if it isn't," Lisa Kavanagh said. "We've already made that claim."

"Claims make me nervous."

"So I've noticed," said Farah Khasnavi, his political analyst.

"Come on Farah," Tor said, "'as far as possible', the great political get-out clause? You know as well as I do that certainties are dangerous."

"But ambiguity can leave a crack big enough for a journo's crow bar."

"And Katherina Molale is Earth's best demolition expert," Lisa muttered "It was a mistake allowing her on this trip."

"You know my answer to that," Tor said, tired of the argument.

"Keep your friends close, but your enemies closer," Lisa said. "I never did find out who said that."

Tor chuckled. Weariness was beginning to bear down on him. "So, everyone, *are* we the first?"

"I've done the research," Farah said. "There are no records anywhere of any human planet-fall on Ia. In fact, no other Alliance race has been given access to the Iaen homeworld. This is an immense honour for Earth."

"And the Iaens' enemy?"

"The Iaens call them the Tal. We know nothing about them. We have no idea who they are or what they look like."

"Another race, native to Ia?" Tor said.

Shu answered this time. "Parallel sentient evolution is not unheard of. There is at least one other Alliance planet on which that has occurred."

"They could be a branch of the Iaens themselves," Farah said. "A different ethnic group or a sub-species of some sort."

"I find it difficult to believe that the Iaens would make war among themselves," Shu said.

"Do we know if there have been any clashes in the past?" Tor asked.

General negatives and shrugs.

"What we do know is that the Iaens seem unable to fight back." This was the first time Claudette Sassi, Tor's

Combined Security Advisor, had spoken. "Which is puzzling, given their level of technological advancement."

"The reason could be cultural," Tor said. "Shu?"

"Possibly. We simply don't know enough about them to make that judgement."

"It seems like a war of conquest, or even genocide to me," Claudette said. "Two races trying to live in peace on one planet? Until recently, our own world was constantly wracked with war and we're all the same species. Despite Shu's example, I can't imagine many instances in which two differing sentient species would co-inhabit peacefully."

"A reasonable assumption, Claudette," Tor said. "But we need to be open to other possibilities, even that the Iaens themselves are the aggressor." He could feel their scepticism "My prime objective is to bring the two parties to the negotiating table. Is that clear? As far as I am concerned, military intervention, however light-touched, is the absolute last resort."

Nods, agreement murmurs.

"We have forgotten, or ignored, one major point, here," Farah said.

"And that is?"

"You hold the deciding vote, Mr Secretary. The pressure to intervene is immense, and not only from the Iaens."

"We are aware of that, Farah –"

"They have offered us more of their technology. The quantum drive was just the start. You know as well as I do, sir, that there are those in the government and the military who are eager to get their hands on whatever the Iaens have for us, at any cost. We need to keep that in mind while we are down there."

"All right. Thank you everyone. Let's prepare ourselves for planet-fall." Tor leaned across to Lisa who was seated next to him. "I want Katherina Molale given free rein."

"Sir, with all due respect –"

"An order Lisa, I don't give many, but I'm giving one now."

"Yes sir." Lisa made to enter the order on her noter then hesitated. "That quote, about keeping our enemies closer, who was it?"

"Joseph Stalin."

Chuckling, Tor turned away and caught a glimpse of Ia; blue, dotted with white cloud and splashed with the brown of mountains. The moment of wonder was snatched away by a hard turn that became a nosedive towards the planet's surface. Why the hell, Tor wondered as the shuddering and roaring began, did they not offer anaesthetic for this as well?

He must have passed-out because suddenly the sky outside was clear blue. They were in level flight and there was a glimpse of distant mountains through the viewport to his left. His ears ached and his nose bled. Someone was throwing-up further back in the cabin and someone else was crying. A man by the sound of it.

I know how you feel, Tor told him silently. Another turn, gentle this time, and a city came into view.

It was unlike any city Tor had seen before. The buildings, presumably they *were* buildings, were thousands of feet high and all identical. Each one resembled the rounded, slightly flattened, shape of a titanic pebble. The dark, grey-blue mottling on their gently curved surfaces heightened the resemblance. The structures were strictly regimented and the gaps between them formed into arrow-straight streets. The regimentation was broken here and there by the occasional plaza. The whole thing reminded him, unnervingly, of a giants' grave yard

The lander dropped lower until it was forced to weave, dizzyingly, between the buildings. Nauseous, white-knuckled and sweating, Tor closed his eyes and hoped for the best. After a few minutes the lander slowed to a halt. It trembled alarmingly as the landing jets fired and Tor fought panic as it dropped towards the ground. At the last moment, the pilot slowed the descent to make the gentlest of touchdowns.

Tor unbuckled his seat restraint. One of the marine

sergeants who had accompanied his party, was already on her feet. She motioned Tor to remain where he was, then headed through the hatch into the forward area. Two of her men stationed themselves by the hatch. Tor heard the heavy drone of the ramp being lowered. It was followed by the heavy bootfalls of the marine detachment. Theirs would be the first human feet to step onto the surface of Ia.

A moment.

"All right, Mr Secretary." The sergeant was back. "All secure."

Tor took a deep breath then left his seat and followed Claudette to the ramp. The plan was for the rest of the delegation to wait at the top until Tor had shaken hands with his Iaen counterpart.

The light was early-evening gold. The air chilled but pleasant and breathable.

Boots crunched as the marines, who were lined-up on either side of the ramp's lower edge, came to attention.

They had made planet-fall in a plaza deep in the city. The square was empty, apart from the lander and the delegation. There was no Iaen welcoming committee. No brass band or pomp. No one. Nothing.

The square was bordered by the huge, pebble-like structures that formed the city. Their summits reared dizzyingly into clear evening sky. Their flanks were smooth with no sign of anything that resembled windows and broken by no visible entrances. The effect of this was to make them seem more monolith than dwelling, totems perhaps, or machines. Whatever they were, Tor felt intimidated by their sheer size and overwhelming *presence*. There was something more than the inanimate here, something that was almost regard. It was as if the buildings watched him.

Judged him.

Tor sensed the sergeant's tension. This had all the hallmarks of a trap.

Then came the sound. A sigh, a hiss. An opening formed at the base of the nearest of the buildings. Again, it was *wrong*, not a door in any sense that Tor understood it, but a tear in the structure's fabric, which further enhanced the sense that the things were organic. A single figure stepped out and set off across the plaza. It was an Iaen. Seven, perhaps almost eight, feet tall, humanoid, hairless. Its flesh was a waxy white colour. Blood vessels were webbed in blue and dark red over its sculptured musculature.

Tor had met Iaens before. Like this one, they looked oddly unfinished, as if they were something hastily fashioned to make themselves acceptable, and perhaps a little intimidating, to humans, although they had never offered any threat.

The Iaen towered over him, arm extended in an incongruously human gesture. Tor accepted the offer and they shook hands. The Iaen's enormous paw enfolded his own. It was warm, its flesh unnervingly smooth.

"Secretary Danielson, I am pleased to meet you." The Iaen's voice was deep and mellow, its Earth-standard perfect and unaccented. "I would like to welcome you to Ia. This is a great day for me."

Me? Not *us?*

"And for humankind," Tor answered. "It is an honour to be here on your world."

"Come." The request was brusque. The Iaen's face registered no particular emotion, or expression.

There was no guard of honour. Instead, a lonely walk across an empty space into the vast and intimidating building from which the Iaen had emerged. Tor did not look back. He trusted that the rest of his delegation was not far behind and that the moment was being caught on the vid-comms of a handful of carefully selected journos.

*

Katherina's mood progressed swiftly from bored to angry. She had, of course, not been selected to witness the historic moment that was a human stepping onto the surface of Ia. Lisa Kavanagh had seen to that. Instead, she was left to kick her heels in the lander. The vessel was confining. The other journos bored her. They were, in her opinion, a mindless flock of forelock-tugging sheep.

She got out of her seat and moved along the aisle, past the card game that had replaced news gathering, and over to the water dispenser. She stared through the open hatch into the forward cabin. All the seats were empty. No chance of slipping off the lander, however. There were marines everywhere. Patience was required. She and the others would be allowed off eventually. Tor would see to that. She would have to wait.

She filled a tumbler with water and moved to the sealed hatch. As she drank, she peered through the port at the strangely uniform buildings.

And saw a marine patrol flyer seemingly wink into existence about a quarter of a mile away.

Bewildered, Katherina watched as the craft was thrown into a tight arc to race back the way it had come.

It vanished.

No, not vanished, exactly. There had been a ripple in the air. The way water, and the reflections it contained, rippled outwards when struck by a pebble.

Katherina stared at the spot from which the flyer had emerged. It was a band of evening-blue sky framed between the flanks of two buildings. What business did a flyer have behind that invisible curtain of liquid air? In fact, why was the flyer here at all? Flyers were not fitted with quantum drives. They were atmospheric aircraft, basic in design and fitted with standard jet-fan engines. They were not built for re-entry and were normally delivered in transporters. Transporters were big. The only starships capable of carrying them were cruisers. There were no cruisers in orbit around Ia.

In fact, there should be no Earth or Alliance ships at all on this side of the quantum tunnel other than the *Kissinger*.

Or any other humans on Ia apart from Tor's delegation, its escort and the embedded journos.

That turn. God knew how many gees it had pulled. The

strain on the flyer's airframe must have been immense. It had been an emergency manoeuvre, one that reeked of an almost comical oh-shit-we-took-a-left-when-we-should-have-taken-a-right panic and do-you-think-they-saw-us desperation.

None of the other journos seemed to have noticed the incident, or if they had, the wrongness of it had not penetrated their thick, sycophantic skulls.

Okay, now Katherina had a mission. She was going over there. She wasn't sure how, but she was going. The need for patience was suddenly bearable, because she required time to come up with a plan.

*

Tor found himself in a vast chamber, lit by a glow that emanated from deep within the surfaces of its huge walls and the distant dome of its ceiling. There were no windows and the only visible door was the one through which Tor had entered with the Iaen. There was no furniture, no chairs, and no table. Other than Tor's greeter, there were no other Iaens present either.

Tor's first impression was that the room was empty, but after a few moments he became aware that the walls were more than simple inorganic boundaries. They were textured and glistened as if made from some fleshy material. The walls were also translucent enough for Tor to see shapes sliding and slithering behind their surfaces. Whatever the shapes were, they were enormous. As to their form; one moment they were serpentine and as vast as dragons, the next, as amorphous as clouds.

There was a snatch of music. Mendelssohn's Violin Concerto.

Christ, not that.

Shape-shifting and vague as they were, their presence was immense. Tor's head began to ache. He felt as nauseous as he had in the lander. He glanced at the others and saw that, for the most part they looked equally as pale and ill as he felt. Well, they would all have to endure this the best they could. There was work to do.

"I'm ready to talk," the Iaen said.

"As are we," Tor said. "But I have a question before we begin."

"Yes?"

"Are you the sole Iaen negotiator, or will we be meeting any other representatives?"

"I am Ia."

Tor was puzzled by the statement. "I'm sorry. I don't…"

Shu moved in close to stage-whisper; "It appears that the Iaen doesn't simply represent the Iaens, he…it embodies them. They are it and it is them."

An impossible concept, as far as Tor was concerned, but he would have to deal with it. "I apologise for any misunderstanding," he said.

The Iaen remained impassive. "Shall we proceed with our negotiation?" it asked.

"Yes, of course," Tor paused for a moment. He was going to be blunt. He needed to remove his own feelings from the words. "I think we should clarify our positions first. Earth, as a member of the Alliance, cannot engage in unilateral military action on behalf of another Alliance member. We value our membership and do not want to jeopardise it in any way."

"Understood."

"There are, however, many on Earth who would support some form of intervention."

"Six of the seven Assembly Chief Secretaries."

"Yes."

"And you have yet to cast your vote."

"That is correct."

"But you are concerned with Earth's responsibilities and obligations to the Alliance."

"We, that is my delegation and I, need more information concerning the nature of the conflict in which you are engaged before I can make my decision. We need to know the identity of the Tal, the origin of the war and the details of any threat they pose to yourself, Earth and the Alliance." He took a breath. "Finally, we need an exact breakdown of what you require of us. I want to assure you that humankind counts you as close friends and are grateful for all that you have done for us as a race. We do want to help you."

"My enemy is the Tal. They are a disease. They threaten my very existence and consequently that of the Alliance and all its members."

"Then why don't you ask for aid from the Alliance? Why just Earth?"

"The Alliance suffers from the malady of all sentient conglomerations; indecision and the pursuance of self-interest. Humankind is the most primitive of all Alliance members and retains a warlike spirit. Your recent intra-species conflicts have sharpened your fighting skills and your military technology is of the highest order. You are the only Alliance race capable of fighting the Tal."

"But what about your own technology? It's far more advanced than ours. Why do you need us?"

The Iaen appeared to consider this for a long time and it occurred to Tor that it might be communicating in some way with the entities in the walls. "My technology is of little use against this particular enemy. It requires your cruder machineries."

Tor glanced at the others, all of whom were managing to stay on their feet despite their obvious physical distress. His own head rang with the hammer blows of an oncoming migraine.

Mendelssohn again.

"All right, look, I think we all need to rest for a while. We seem to be having problems acclimatising to your world." It was this building. Outside everyone had felt fine, apart for the lingering effects of planetfall. "I'm sorry."

"Of course."

"I must reiterate my personal position, which is that Earth cannot undertake direct military action against the Tal without Alliance approval. For me, that is non-negotiable."

"This is a complex issue. The Alliance itself is under threat. If I fall to the Tal, the Alliance will disintegrate and fall with me. It is my presence and influence that holds the Alliance together."

"All right. There must be avenues we can explore here," Tor said. His headache had intensified into a painful, piercing throb, as if a nail was being pounded into his skull in time with his heartbeat. Thinking was difficult, his thoughts muddied. "Other forms of assistance that we can render."

The shadows in the walls writhed and twisted. Tor blinked. There were dancers in there, silhouettes that waltzed into view then dissolved into cloud, only to reform into a crowd, a cityscape, a shadow.

He saw a life-support pod, his wife, seated beside it, head bowed, her hand on the glass. She turned to look at him. He whispered her name and almost broke down again.

The image dissolved and something immense slid along the inside face of the wall then flicked back into the opaque cloudiness of its interior.

We know, it said. *We see and we know.*

"…manner of assistance?"

Tor started. "I'm sorry." It was becoming difficult to speak. Pain beat through his skull. He shivered, dank with sweat.

"I'm sorry?"

"You offered me *other forms of assistance.*"

"Ah, yes, of course. My apologies, I was thinking of advisors. People who can train your…you…" But wasn't that involvement? One remove from boots on the ground, perhaps, but soldiers and weapons, and side-taking nonetheless. He needed to sharpen up. He was backing himself into a corner. "I need more information…I need to meet with the Tal."

He heard a groan, then Shu crumpled to the floor beside him and all hell broke loose. The marine sergeant rushed in, shouting orders into her throat-comm as she did so. Farah stumbled away, holding her head and muttering incoherently. Marines appeared and quickly formed a defensive arc about the delegation. Their weapons were drawn, many aimed at the Iaen, others at the things in the walls.

Tor yelled at them to stand down, but the sergeant's was the only voice they listened to and she was yelling at them to get everyone out.

Now!

One of the marines helped Shu to his feet, another put her arms about Farah's shoulders and bustled her towards the door. The Advisor sobbed uncontrollably. Tor caught a final glimpse of the dancers who had returned to the walls and were swinging each other round faster and faster. The sight of it was maddening.

*

Katherina's patience ran out as the Iaen sun dropped low and turned bloody. She needed to get off this lander and she needed to find out what the hell was going on in the southern part of the city from where the patrol flyer had made its brief appearance. The oncoming dusk and subsequent dark would provide all the cover she needed, but she was trapped in here because the passenger cabin hatches were locked.

She wandered to the forward cabin again. The security agent was nowhere in sight. There was, however, a solitary marine slouched on one of the seats and staring at a vid-palm.

"Sorry ma'am, you can't come in here." The marine wasn't as indolent as he had appeared.

"I know, but I'm bored with the rest of the idiots back there. I just wanted to talk to someone from the real world."

"I understand, but –"

"How's the service these days."

"What do you mean?"

Katherina rolled up the sleeve of her overall. The marine took a step closer and when he saw the tattoo his polite hostility dissolved into wonder.

"You were in the 14th? A Hellbringer?"

Katherina nodded. "The very same. Hey, where are your buddies?"

"Sleeping up in the control room. This planet's friendly turf, ma'am. I don't know why we're here at all."

"To keep us journos from causing trouble."

He chuckled. "That's about it."

He was young and skinny. He took another look at her tattoo. "Isn't that the sigil for the Antarctic Campaign?"

"It is."

"You were *there*?"

"From beginning to end."

She recoiled from the memory. The water war had been apocalyptic. Its climactic battle for the Antarctic, an abattoir. Only twenty-two years ago, so recent and yet so far into her history. It was a darkness that boiled into her dreams and sometimes her waking moments.

"I'm sorry I was rude, ma'am."

"You were doing your job. So, back to my question; how is the service these days?"

"There's a lot of peace."

"You don't sound too pleased about that."

"Well, I am of course, no one wants another war, but I've been trained to fight. I guess, if I'm honest, me and my buddies would like to get into at least one brawl before our time's up. I feel like some kind of a fraud, a whole year of service and I've never fired a shot in anger."

"Pray you don't."

"You know what war is like. Me and my buddies don't."

"You're right. Unfortunately."

"Coffee?"

"Yes, thanks."

"Take a seat. Make yourself comfortable ma'am."

Katherina did so. The marine was back quickly. "What *was* it like?" he said as he handed her the drink. "I hope you don't mind me asking. I mean, if you don't want to talk about it…"

"That's okay…hey, what's your name? Oh, I see it, Nakamura."

"Nak. That's what my buddies call me, ma'am."

"And you can call me Katherina."

They drank in companionable silence for a moment. Then Katherina spoke. "I'll answer your question because you're a marine. That makes us brother and sister."

"Thanks ma…Katherina."

She didn't want to talk about it, but it was a means to an end and this kid needed to hear it. "Well, it was cold and it was dark."

Dark because it was as if the sky had drawn the clouds across its face to hide its eyes from the horror below. The cloud's underbelly was splashed orange and red by the task-force bombardment. The gales drowned the relentless hammering of the guns and boom of impact. The sea was a violent, sick-making landscape of ever-shifting, cobalt mountains. Everything on the deck of the ship was draped in ice. Descending the nets to get into the landing craft had taken scores of marines even before the fighting began and for those who made it into the boats, the journey shore-wards was a terrifying roller coaster that hurled the craft upwards then wrenched it back down into the ocean's spray-laden belly.

Then, sick, cold and frightened they hit the beach which was not a beach at all, but a wasteland of snow and rock.

Hatch open, ramp down. Out, come on, out, out, out!

Marines crumpled and fell, bleeding, into the freezing surf. Others made it onto the ice and shingle before their flesh and bones were punched out of their bodies by machine-gun bullets or their limbs were torn-off by mortar shells.

Sergeant Katherina Molale was first out of her craft. She ran. There was nothing else she could do and nowhere else to go. Her uniform, helmet and pack were heavy. Her legs stiff and unresponsive. The rifle was a dead weight in her hands. She ran at an enemy whose identity she wasn't sure of. One fundamentalist group or another. Some rebel band who denied the authority of the newly-installed Assembly and sought to claim land and water and food as their own. They were the enemy of Order. They were anarchists, chaos-bringers.

This icy hell was their last outpost. This was where their power was to be broken.

Katherina ran through the white-hot, iron blizzard and was so astounded to find herself alive when she reached the parapet of the enemy trenches, she lost all fear and feeling and later, all memory of how she helped carve a bloody swathe through the equally startled defenders to silence their guns.

"You know what damaged me the most?"

Nak looked pale. He shrugged. He didn't know.

"Discovering that the enemy were human beings. Like me, and you. There were men, women, old folk, even kids manning those defences. All they wanted was to be left in peace."

"But surely, order was needed," Nak said. "You couldn't leave any rebels or anarchists alive. The Assembly had to be ruthless to save humankind."

Katherina bit down on her counter-argument. She needed Nak's cooperation. "I guess you're right," she said instead. "You know something, I could do with some air. Talking about the war...I feel kind of sick."

"I'm sorry, but I'm not supposed to let anyone out of the lander."

"Come on, just for a few minutes. A small favour, one marine to another. I'm not going anywhere."

Nak appeared to agonise for a moment then come to a decision. "Okay, but just for a couple of minutes."

"Two minutes. I promise."

He opened the hatch and there was the ramp down which the delegation had walked a few hours earlier. Katherina stepped onto it and saw, immediately, that something was happening. There was a platoon of marines, weapons hot, crouched as if ready for a fight. They were formed into an arc about the entrance to the building into which Tor and his delegation had disappeared an hour before. She heard shouts. Figures

22

emerged; Farah Ghusnavi, supported by a marine.

"What the hell?" Nak was beside her, rifle in hand. "They need help. Stay here." He ran down the ramp and headed for his comrades. Others began to exit the building. Katherina caught a glimpse of Tor, supported by Security Agents, looking dishevelled, holding his head as if in pain.

A story was unfolding right here. She should stay.

No, the sheep would pick that up. She had an exclusive to chase. Katherina dropped onto her back then quietly and efficiently rolled over the side of the ramp and landed lightly on her feet under the lander's belly.

The light was fading fast. There were plenty of dark spots and only a few yards behind the lander, the first of the titanic Iaen buildings. Beyond them, the arrow-straight street was dipped in vast pools of deep shadow. Katherina stepped onto the planet's surface. It was hard and dusty. No tarmac or concrete. The ground had simply been levelled and nothing more. She knew she should feel guilty, using Nak like this. She would speak up for him when she returned, use the tattoo to charm his CO (no marine, no matter how hard-assed, would ever disrespect a Hellbringer who fought in the Antarctic Campaign) and put the blame squarely on herself.

She waited. It looked as if the whole delegation and its escort was on its way back to the lander. Everyone seemed shaken.

Katherina broke into a light run, and headed for the shadows.

Running because there was nothing else she could do…

She reached the first building unobserved, or, at least, unchallenged. The vast, identical structures towered over her like titanic standing stones. Their silence was, somehow, *loud*. It pressed-in and smothered her. It roared in her ears and pulsed through her head.

Trying to shake off her unease, she consulted her own palm-pad and followed its eCompass due south. The shadows deepened and the silence grew louder.

*

A conference room had been set-up in the lander's hold. Its curved, tunnel-like walls and low ceiling made it cramped, hot and claustrophobic. But it was home. Coffee was served, food brought in. The marine company's medic checked everyone over.

"Where's Lisa?" Tor asked. His headache had eased a little. The pain left him exhausted.

"She was waylaid by the marine commander as we came aboard," Farah said.

"Damn it. I need to speak with her. I don't want the journos all over this. Not yet. We may have offended the Iaens by walking out the way we did. I don't want the press making it worse."

"I'll fetch her," Sergeant Olsen said. Although pale and obviously shaken, she seemed the least affected of all of them.

"Thanks," Tor said. Someone placed a mug of coffee in his hands. Even the smell of it was a comfort. He noticed that he still trembled. "Let's eat and get some coffee down our throats while we talk. Firstly, I want to know if you're all okay."

General affirmatives from everyone. Although no one looked particularly healthy.

"What happened in there?" Tor said. "Any ideas? Shu?"

"Many people have found the Iaens intimidating. Stepping onto their world seems to have magnified that sense of...of...dislocation."

"I think it's more than that," Tor said. "We've always assumed that the beings we've interacted with up till now were the Iaens themselves, but I'm beginning to wonder."

"I agree. I would say that, up until now, we have only met part of who they are."

"It felt as if the building was alive," Farah said. She sounded badly shaken. "Whatever it is, it knew my deepest fears and weaknesses."

"Sentient?" Shu asked.

"Possibly," Farah said. "Could it be that the Iaen we've been used to seeing and interacting with are a separate species, or part of a life cycle, the larval stage, for instance? What we saw in the walls, or even the buildings themselves are the adults."

"Possibly. Or vice versa. Or..." Shu hesitated, as if uncomfortable with what he was about to say. "They're a trinity."

"Like the Christian God?" Tor said.

"Yes. The Iaen with whom we are interacting is the physical, the Son, if you like. He addresses the Iaen race as *I*. He is the Word made flesh. The entities we glimpsed within the walls, the Father perhaps, the true Iaen. And the force by which these two components are knit together, the Spirit."

"A feasible comparison, I suppose," Tor said. "None of us have a better theory. However, I don't think we should take your theory to its inevitable conclusion, Shu. The Iaens are not gods."

Lisa returned. She looked harassed and angry. "Mr Secretary, it's Molale, she's disappeared."

"How the hell did she manage that, Lisa?"

"Sweet-talked some green-behind-the-ears private and dazzled him with her Hellbringer tattoos apparently. He's in serious trouble; dereliction of duty."

"The poor lad never stood a chance," Tor said. "Send his CO to me and I'll get him off the hook."

"And what are you going to do about Ms Molale's refusal to obey orders?" Shu demanded.

"Nothing," Tor replied. "I'm not her boss. What's she going to find anyway? This is a big city and, as far as we can tell, its streets are deserted. The war isn't taking place here."

"With all due respect, Mr Secretary, I find your response to this crisis, somewhat cavalier."

"With all due respect to you, Lisa, this isn't a crisis. I'll answer for the consequences. If Katherina uncovers something that smells bad then it will be something we need to know about."

"You make it sound as if she's working for you as a spy," Lisa countered. "That raises ethical concerns."

"Think what you want. More importantly than worrying over errant journos, we have to find out exactly what the Iaen-Tal war is about and who the enemy are."

"And where?"

"Yes, thank you, Farah. I'd like to meet with the Tal."

"It's doubtful that the Iaens will let us," Farah said.

"I strongly advise against it, sir" Shu said. "We have no information about them whatsoever. Until we do, we should avoid contact at all costs. There is another aspect of this to consider. We've already seen that the Iaens are more unlike ourselves than we realised. Their concept of war might also be different to ours, in fact, it may even be incomprehensible to us, which would explain the lack of smoke and noise."

"Except that they seem to believe that we are more suited to fight the Tal than they are, so they must be a physical, comprehensible enemy."

"The Iaens gave us interstellar travel," Farah said, "and yet they can't fight a war on their own planet. That doesn't make sense."

"Have you seen any technology here?" Shu asked.

No, Tor realised, he hadn't. "This is a big planet, and this is just one city."

"True, but something feels wrong."

"Yes," Tor said. "It does."

*

She wasn't alone. Someone, a woman as far as Katherina could tell, was walking towards her along the empty, silent street. It was dusk. The figure was indistinct. There was no hiding from it, so she steeled herself for a direct challenge. She took a step. The figure did the same. She raised her right hand. The figure copied the gesture.

"Jesus," Katherina whispered and laughed ruefully. "Idiot."

The figure was herself. A reflection, presumably.

Reflected on what?

She noticed the shimmer then. Faint but there, in the air, on the surfaces of the giant Iaen buildings, the same shimmering effect that had accompanied the appearance and disappearance of the marine flyer.

So, if this other Katherina Molale wasn't a doppelganger from some parallel universe, she was indeed a reflection and the shimmer acted as a giant mirror. Did that mean that what appeared to be a panorama of the city beyond this point was, in fact, a mirror image of what was already there? If so, it was a remarkably life-like one. It was, she knew, an outrageous idea, but the only explanation she could come up with at that moment.

So, what lay behind the mirror?

The flyer had passed through, apparently without hazard, although, for all Katherina knew, it might have been shattered into a million burning fragments on its return passage or sent to some other time or universe.

Damn it, she had to know. That was her job, wasn't it? Journalist, enquirer, truth-seeker, interfering mischief-maker and spy?

She steeled herself and once more raised her hand. The primitive within her yelled at her that she could die. It was like reaching towards the bare terminal of some high voltage device. It was madness.

She thrust her hand forward, winced and waited for death, injury or pain.

There was none. There was nothing. No sensation, no tingle, no electric shock or burning agony. Nothing.

Deep breath.

A step.

Through.

Again nothing. No pain, no cold, no heat. It was if the screen did not exist.

She opened her eyes, only now realising that she had clenched them shut.

In the first moment she believed it to be a flashback, some scene from her five-year service with the marines.

What she saw disorientated her. Surely it was an illusion, or perhaps she had been right about being catapulted into some other universe. But as the moment raced by, she realised that it was real. The noise, the smell, the crunch of debris under her feet, the taste and stink of smoke.

The city beyond the screen was a battlefield.

*

A snatch of music startled Tor awake. As he opened his eyes to the darkness, the music fragmented into his own heartbeat. He lay motionless, and there, vivid against the black was Eva, violin tucked under her chin. The long delicate fingers of her left hand were curled about its neck, the fingers of her right held the bow so lightly it seemed as if *it* was guiding *her* hand. The music was beautiful, Mendelssohn's Violin Concerto, the last piece he had seen her play. It had moved him far beyond paternal admiration and love for his daughter. Her interpretation of the work and the emotional fervour of her playing had pierced his soul and he had bled willingly.

The image faded and no matter how much he tried to cling to it and hold it to himself, she greyed and merged into the dark and was gone.

A moment. That was what it had been. A moment that could only be grasped while it existed.

Tor sat up in his seat – which doubled as a bunk – and looked out of the lander's viewport. The city, now silvered by Ia's immense moon, was still and peaceful. The city was unlit, a jumble of gigantic softly glowing shapes that stretched as far as he could see. The sky was littered with stars. No familiar constellations here, although, the longer he looked, the more shapes and patterns he could see. He knew that human colonists quickly created new constellations in their skies. Order must prevail, he mused. Humans cannot cope with chaos.

His daughter's illness, however, was a chaos he could not control. The mess that was his marriage, on the other hand, was a chaos he had unleashed.

He had to stop this. He was sinking towards another breakdown. There would be time for grief later. He had a mission. He had humankind's future in his hands. A convulsive laugh, or was it sob, broke through at the thought. *He* had the future of humankind in *his* hands?

Not for much longer. This was his last mission. He could not do this anymore. The strain was immense. Politics had devoured him for the last thirty years of his life. Now he needed to serve himself and his family. He was still married, which meant that he had a chance, albeit a slim one. He would finish this job and go home. He would try to persuade his wife that they should work through the pain and, perhaps, find love once more.

And Katherina?

Bringing her along was always a risk.

He still loved her. There was no doubt about that. This time, however, he would not act on the feeling. This time he would ride the wave of hurt and go home to his family.

She had been part of the journo pack that had followed him on his first missions as Chief Secretary. She was the one who enlivened his press conferences with awkward questions. She was the one whom Lisa always tried to shut down. She was the one Tor noticed and looked forward to sparring with.

There was a meeting with the Alliance on a nasty little planet called Cressida. Nasty for humans that is. For the aggrieved Alliance member-race who were the reason for the summit, it was a little slice of heaven. The talks were held in one of Cressida's remote human-owned mining complexes. The Iaens were present, and this was the first time Tor had encountered them in the flesh.

Late one evening, if there could be such a differentiation between time periods on Cressida, Tor had sneaked down to the miners' bar. He wore a borrowed colonist's overall and was escorted only by one security agent. He needed to escape the intensity of the summit and the clamouring neediness of his entourage. He needed to be as alone as it was possible for him to be.

Katherina was there already. She recognised him, of course, and promised not to give him away. They drank. They talked. Katherina was incisive, irreverent, intelligent and funny. He loved her voice. He couldn't keep from seeking her stare with his own. She touched his knee and that seemingly accidental contact was electric.

They went back to his rooms.

It had taken a while for the guilt to hit. For those first few days it had been a delirium of passion and what he believed to be love. But then, one night, in the unforgiving small hours, the crippling Truth slammed into him. He called her in for an interview. He wanted to end it, but when he saw her, he couldn't.

The public would never know. The Assembly had re-established deference for one's betters. When Tor arrived home, he discovered that such deference did not extend to family. The storm was terrible. Annika was wounded and Tor feared that her wounds would never heal.

There was only one remedy, demanded by Annika, commanded by the Assembly.

Alone again, Tor stood in Katherina's apartment, held her tight and felt the shudder of her sobs. The utter desolation carved into her face when he finally stepped back and turned for the door, burned itself into his memory and still haunted his dreams.

Annika stayed. He suspected it was not only because the Assembly expected it of her. Marriage was sacred. There was no other choice. Duty, it might be, yet Tor was certain that he could still see a glint of love trapped within the ice and steel of Annika's resentment.

*

Katherina had found the war.

Half-crouched, frozen by flashback and shock, she glimpsed it through the swirls of smoke and in the dancing orange-yellow light of countless fires. She saw it in the stroboscopic flashes of explosions. She was battered by the relentless crash and roar of it, a noise so brutal it punched into her and doubled her over. It clamped her hands over her ears. She tasted it in the smoke, dust and soot-filled air. She smelled it. The stink was the cloying, sickly-sweet perfume of necrosis and burned flesh.

It was that smell that was most evocative. The smell that brought the flashback, the fear and barely restrained panic and made her want to run because –

-there was nothing else she could do and nowhere else to go.

She stood just inside the reflective force-field. It seemed as if she was half a mile or so behind the battlefront. The burgeoning dark was lit jaggedly by a steady rhythm of artillery flashes and washed with the uncertain dance of firelight. Her immediate surroundings were a jumble of burned-out, Iaen buildings, many of them reduced to charred stumps only ten or twenty feet high. There were wrecked vehicles and there were bodies, dark shapes in the gloom. The smell of them could not be hidden, and familiar as it was to Katherina, it slithered into her and made her gag and retch. The corpses all looked to be human.

She forced herself to move and picked her way cautiously to the closest of them. She crouched again, to examine the body. A fire burned nearby. Her face was bathed in its heat. The corpse was lit by its glow. It wore a marine uniform, burned and torn, but recognisable enough. That was the only part of it that was recognisable.

When she straightened, Katherina realised that the wrecked and abandoned vehicles were marine crawlers.

Katherina unhooked the micro-comm from its socket implant in her left palm and snapped it into the outlet on the left breast pocket of her overall. She waited for the green LED to wink into life then set off towards the nearest of the artillery flashes, hoping to God that the gunners were marines and that she was making for the human lines.

As she closed on the positions, she began to see men and vehicles silhouetted against a backdrop of oily flame. She passed a group of exhausted soldiers, who looked to have found refuge from the battle in the lee of a partly demolished Iaen building. Their heads were down, as if asleep. One of them was on his knees and stared sightlessly into the distance, flames reflected in his wide-open eyes. All seemed oblivious to her presence.

The fire up ahead erupted suddenly into a vast orange-black inferno. Katherina felt a wave of heat, then choked on the second wave, which also carried the stink of burning. The marines appeared to be fighting their way into the city and from the destruction she had seen so far, systematically razing its buildings to the ground.

Figures hurried towards her from what she assumed to be the line. She drew back into the shadow of a burnt-out tank. The figures carried stretchers and were making for a large field hospital crawler that had taken up station a few hundred yards back from the fighting. As her senses attuned themselves to the noise and erratic light, she became aware of more vehicles and activity. She had reached the rear positions. Ammunition stores, a field hospital, resting men and reserve units waiting their turn. No one appeared to have noticed her.

A sudden salvo of cannon fire and mortar-flash erupted and the marine assault seemed re-energised. Arcs of white-hot ordnance were blasted into the dark to the right of the burning building. Opposing flashes of tracer fire indicated that the marines were not having it all their own way.

A magnesium flare burst a couple of hundred feet above the battle. In its sudden and stark light, Katherina saw the strange nature of the ruin around her more clearly than before. The damaged buildings looked as if they had been torn open rather than blasted by shells. And they bled. Stains ran from the savage wounds ripped into their flanks. Dried now, but blood-like. It was as if the fabric of the structures was fibrous, organic even. The roast-flesh stink given out as they burned, reinforced the impression.

Katherina moved forward. She stayed low, hugged the shadows. The light lost its coherence once more as the flare died. She was close enough to hear voices now; shouted orders, the screams of the wounded.

She dropped to her belly, once more in the lee of a shattered war-machine, so ruined it was beyond identification. There was a corpse only a few feet from where she lay. Its face was turned towards her; eyes closed, as if sleeping. Its upper body looked unscathed, armour intact, helmet in place, but there was little other than organic mess from the waist down. Shaking, trying to blank out the dead marine, Katherina unhooked the micro-comm from her chest and scanned the scene in front of her. She added a commentary. There was no point in trying to speak quietly.

"I am Katherina Molale, a Redman News Agency Freelancer. I am on Ia as part of the embedded press pack covering negotiations between Chief Secretary Danielson and the Iaens. We were led to believe that the delegation, its accompanying marine detachment, and its embedded journo-pack were the first humans ever to set foot on this planet. It seems that we have been misled. Earth is already involved in a war on its surface, possibly with the Tal, whom the Iaens claim to be their enemy. You are witnessing a major assault by a large marine force. The marine equipment includes heavy weapons that were definitely not brought here by the *Kissinger*. The battle has been concealed behind some form of reflecting energy shield. This action begs the questions of whether Secretary Danielson is aware of this flagrant breach of Alliance protocols? Also, who sanctioned this action?

"I'm going forward, closer to the fighting. I'm —"

A nearby armoured crawler exploded. The world shook. The noise punched into Katherina's eardrums and drove the air from her chest. She hugged the ground, then looked up. The marines were running back from the front line. Some were on fire. Dark, struggling figures stumbled over the bodies of the fallen and the devastation they had wrought as they tried to escape whatever was coming. It looked like a rout.

The first of them blundered past Katherina. No one paid her any heed. The heavy cannon on one of the reserve crawlers behind where she crouched, opened up. Tracer sliced overhead then a rocket that flared bright, went dim, seemed to disappear, then hit its target and exploded.

They came.

Their vanguard poured through the broken lines, firing machine guns from the hip.

They.

The enemy. The Tal.

Who were human marines.

*

She kept filming. The attackers were closing in fast. The marine position was about to be overrun. The enemy force seemed limitless, an uncountable horde, a dark mass that steamrollered through the defenders' fire and threatened to crush everything in its path. She should run. Now.

Too late.

One of the attackers headed straight towards her. Katherina watched him approach, transfixed, confused, all vestiges of her training gone. The marine stumbled to a halt and raised his weapon. Katherina kneeled slowly, arms extended crucifix-style and hoped the soldier understood the gesture of surrender.

She realised that she was holding her breath. She stared into the barrel of its rifle. The tiny black eye was redolent with latent violence. The exit point for the bullet that would kill her.

Waiting.

"Up."

At first the word, clearly spoken in Standard, did not register with her.

Up.

The soldier was close now. One side of his face and

uniform were in shadow, the other was bathed in the orange glow of the fires that burned around them. The uncertain light was bright enough for Katherina to notice something odd about the weapon. It looked like a standard marine automatic, but it was *fleshy*, as if it was an organic copy. It was, she knew, still a rifle and its bullets, bone or metal, could still kill her. Katherina kept her arms raised. See, unarmed. I'm your prisoner. She prayed that the micro-comm was still running.

Don't die on me now. I need to get this. All of it.

The fake-marine regarded her for a moment then, in a sudden, oddly graceful movement, grabbed her left arm and yanked her to her feet.

She saw him properly then.

He was unformed. His face an empty representation of a human face, basic, rough-hewn and unfinished. It was as if some poorly skilled sculptor had attempted human features in clay then given up before it was complete. She saw, also, that his uniform was webbed with vessels and was joined to his flesh, or more probably, part of it.

Did this mean that her captor was a Tal? Were they shape-changers? If so, they were impressionists rather than portrait artists.

The Tal shoved her into motion and they headed back the way he had come. His grip was brutally tight and his pace punishing. Katherina stumbled in its wake, desperate to keep up because she was convinced that if she fell the being would simply drag her over the ground. She was frightened. These hostiles did not seem disposed to mercy towards their prisoners.

The sounds of war rumbled and thrummed every side. She had no idea what was happening, whether the assault had been contained, or if the Tal were, even now, breaking through the force field and out into the unscathed part of the city.

More of the Tal joined Katherina and her captor on their withdrawal from the front line. None of them acknowledged her. She noticed that most were wounded but received no help from their comrades. They simply dragged themselves along, some on their hands and knees. She saw one fall, ignored, then stepped over and around.

More of them fell, others limped on. One of them, ahead of her, clung to a shattered arm with his other hand. She felt pity for them, even though they were the enemy and despite the ugly rawness of their faces and the deadness in their featureless black eyes.

As she trudged deeper into the battle-broken city, they met other fake marines, heading for the front line, vast numbers of them. There were also groups of crudely drawn women and children among their ranks. A masterstroke of psychological warfare. What human soldier would be willing to fire both on their own and on defenceless civilians?

The area through which they passed had obviously been fought over many times. The stink of decaying bodies, the burned-out hulks of crawlers, a crashed flyer that lay crumpled, huge and incongruous in the street between two relatively undamaged buildings, all pointed to prolonged, and major, contact between the two forces.

Exhausted, her arm numb, her shoulder aching, Katherina wanted to stop and rest. Her captor seemed tireless, so she stumbled on and hoped that their trek would be over before she collapsed.

They left the battle zone. The structures here were relatively unscathed. The light was no longer the uncertain flicker of flame and explosion but a soft glow that emanated from the buildings themselves. They were identical to the ones beyond the barrier, except that the patterning on the building's flanks was no longer the pebble-like swirls of pastel colour she had seen on the other side of the force-field, but a red and blue webbing that resembled a network of blood vessels. Katherina's captor yanked her round and hauled her towards the entrance to the nearest of them.

She found herself in a tunnel, lit, like the building's exterior, by a glow from within the walls. The walls themselves were textured and ribbed, which gave them the same organic look as the Tal's rifle. Despite the light, it was quickly claustrophobic and Katherina's fear threatened to dissolve into panic. She wanted to scream and beg for release. She was trapped here. She was alone and cut-off. She was being dragged further and further from any hope of salvation. The weight of the structure bore down on her. The air was thick. She was confined, helpless, driven, against her will, deeper and deeper into the building's belly. She was exhausted by physical exertion, shock and by fear.

The tunnel opened abruptly into a large chamber. The space gave only momentary relief, because no matter how high the ceiling or distant the walls, she was still interred deep inside the structure, a long way behind enemy lines.

The chamber was filled with fake marines and more of the women and children. They sat or lay on its floor, unmoving and staring directly ahead. Again, no one tended the wounded. Not one of them spoke. The silence was unnerving.

Katherina noticed that the walls were blistered with large, fluid-filled sacs. Inside, shadowed into silhouette by the sacs' translucent surfaces, were shapes that looked to be foetuses in various states of growth, from tiny, smudged commas to fully developed adults. The Tal were created and birthed, it seemed, by the building itself.

Something changed.

As she watched the floor began to fissure. Red light seeped from the wounds to paint the Tal bloody. Katherina watched, and wondered if this was some form of healing given to the wounded. But then she saw the first of the wounded melt away.

Melted.

The Tal's body collapsed and merged with the softening, lava-like surface. the floor. He made no protest or put up any struggle. He was not the only one. More of the Tal who had returned to the building were being absorbed by the building. Katherina wondered if they comprehended what was happening to them. Did they have any sense of self or understand who and what they were. None of them struggled or uttered a sound throughout the whole process. The Tal wounded were like fallen leaves in autumn, discarded then reclaimed in order to feed the new growth.

The effect was spreading outwards from its epicentre. Katherina pressed herself against the wall. The floor on which she stood had softened but there was a solidity a few inches below. Then in a sudden, and graceful, movement, the Tal spun about and grabbed her tight to himself. His arms were locked about her. She could barely breathe. She couldn't move. Their feet were deep in slime as he dragged her out towards the epicentre of the horror.

Frantic now, she thrashed and twisted and fought but the Tal's grip was a vice.

God, *over her face*. She couldn't see. The stuff was slithering into her ears, her nostrils, forcing itself down her throat.

She was going to die. This wasn't how she wanted it to end.

At some point, she felt the Tal melt away. She tried to hold onto him. She didn't care that he had brought this upon her. She needed him. He was her connection to the world outside this prison of darkness and choking suffocation, but now he was gone.

The end would start soon, the tearing and dissolving pain was about to begin. She tensed for the agony of shredded tissue and crushed organs.

At any moment.

She gagged as the liquid floor poured down her throat and screamed silently at its burning invasion of her tear ducts. She wanted to die now. She wanted it over.

*

"Before we consider any offer of aid, military or otherwise, we need to know more about your enemy."

It was early morning, barely light. Tired from lack of sleep, Tor was resigned to a long day of will-crushing intransigence from the Iaen side. There would be no negotiation. The Iaens wanted military support. Tor was unwilling to cast his vote in favour of such a move. The hours would unwind. The delegation would suffer discomfort which would turn into illness. A break would be called. Nothing would be achieved. Tor did not want to be here. He no longer cared about the upward trajectory of his career. He wanted to go home to his wife and to his daughter before it was too late.

The delegation had returned to the vast, empty space within the Iaen building. Tor glimpsed the snake-like shadows in the walls. As it did yesterday, his unease deepened quickly. His concentration was stolen by that same sense of being watched and *explored.* He prayed to whoever might be listening that he would be able to keep it under control. His head ached. His mouth was dry. He had already seen the dancers in the walls. He had already heard the music. This time, however, it would be different. This time he was prepared.

"The Tal are my enemy," the Iaen said.

"Yes, I understand that, but *who* are they?"

"An alien race."

Promising.

"From where? Do you know their origin, what they want?"

"They are aggressive and expansionist. They are barbaric and they are ruthless."

All this sounded like propaganda, which was strange coming from the lips of an Iaen. Propaganda or not, none of it was of any use whatsoever to Tor.

"Where are they from?" Tor's burgeoning unease was making him impatient. He must fight it and remain calm and polite.

"I cannot tell you."

"Does that mean that you don't know?"

"I cannot tell you."

Tor sighed, waited a moment then continued. "Is there any way we could meet with the Tal? Could you engineer a cease fire?"

A vain hope, Tor knew, but he had to try. He had no capacity for subtlety while in this room. The dancers were dragging his attention from the talks. His headache was growing worse. He could hear Farah murmuring to herself. Shu obsessively polished and repolished his spectacles.

"I have more to give," the Iaen said. It obviously did not intend to discuss talks with the enemy.

"For which, we are grateful," Tor answered, dripping every remaining ounce of diplomatic syrup he possessed into his voice.

"Gratitude will not save me from the Tal." The Iaen countered. Then added; "Nor will it save Earth."

The statement turned Tor's blood to ice. This was new. He glanced at the others, who were all suddenly focussed on the Iaen, all discomfort apparently forgotten. The threat posed by the enigmatic, villainous Tal was suddenly visceral. It bore down on his family. As if there could be something worse than the monster already ravaging Eva's body and soul.

"Are you telling me that Earth is under threat from the Tal?"

"I am."

"Why weren't we warned about this earlier?"

"There was no need."

"No need..." Tor realised that he was losing his temper, losing control. "You have to tell us who they are."

"Only if you agree to help us fight them."

*

"They're lying." The accusation was unthinkable.

The delegation was back outside in the plaza. The sky was clear, the light a rich gold, the sun low but strong enough to warm the dawn chill. Tor had called a halt to the meeting so they could discuss the Iaen's warning.

"That is a serious accusation," Shu said. "A dangerous one too. The Iaens are incapable of dishonesty. They are the most god-like race we have encountered so far."

"Gods lie." Tor was not interested in religious claptrap. "Read your mythology. Gods are scheming and petty. Gods are –"

"The Iaens have never been known to lie to us before," Farah said. She sounded anxious, unnerved. "And if that is the case, the Tal, whoever or whatever they are, really do pose a threat to Earth, and perhaps the Alliance itself. We have to get a message back –"

"No," Tor said. "We need to know more."

"You really doubt the Iaens?" Shu said. "Our allies and friends. A race who lifted us up and gave us, *freely* gave us, the key to the stars?" He shook his head and turned away as if exasperated beyond endurance by Tor's obstinacy. A moment later he swung back. "And now they have promised us another gift. We can't afford to refuse. The Tal are the Iaen's enemy which makes them *our* enemy. We have to help our friends. We have to give them…give them…" His frustration appeared to have finally robbed him of speech.

"Give them what?" Tor demanded. "Worship? Our souls? Listen to me, Shu, the Iaens are not God. They are a sentient race. They are mortal and they are fallible." He pushed back on his anger. His self-control was fraying at its edges. He needed to calm down and reclaim his professionalism. "We are going back inside, and we are turning their own conditions back on them. No meeting with the Tal, means no more discussion of military aid. No give on Iaens' side means we return to the lander and we leave."

"With all due respect Mr Secretary, we must be careful not to offend the Iaens." Shu again. "These people are our friends."

"Are they? They have made no concessions to our well-being. They are not negotiating but simply repeating the same demands over and over again. What's your opinion, Farah?" Tor asked.

"I would also counsel against such a rigid approach," Farah said. "The Iaens can be sensitive. We can't afford to jeopardise our relationship."

"All right, thank you. Your concerns are noted, but I'm sick of the Iaens' refusal to answer my questions and their reluctance to even discuss a meeting with the Tal. So now *I* am going to make some demands."

"Sir, meeting with an enemy force engaged in war is never going to be easy," Farah said.

"We're neutral. We have made no promises to the Iaens. We are not yet the Tal's enemy. I believe that we can pull this off. It might even bring about a ceasefire. At the very least, it will demonstrate to the Alliance that we've explored every avenue. We need to visit the combat zones. We need evidence that a war is actually taking place and we need to understand who the hell they are fighting and who we are being asked to fight on their behalf."

"All right, but we should clarify on our approach," Farah said. "We are asking to see the conflict for ourselves and gain more knowledge of the Tal and the threat they pose. Walking away from the negotiation is our weapon. Agreed?"

All agreed. Tor led the delegation back into the building. The oppression hit him the moment he stepped into the inner chamber. Pain pulsed through his head. He felt dizzy and queasy. The shapes in the walls added to his unease and discomfort. He wanted them to stop moving and to show themselves. Their restlessness made him sick.

"Before you continue," the Iaen said. "I will reveal our gift to you."

"This isn't the moment –"

"It *is* the right moment," Shu said. "We're at an impasse. Perhaps it will provide a breakthrough."

Tor sighed wearily. "All right."

"I need one of you to step forward." Dear God, now the Iaen sounded like a stage magician. "And that person must trust me implicitly."

Before Tor could answer, or volunteer himself, Shu stepped forward. "What do I have to do?"

"As I said. You have to trust me," the Iaen said. "Come, here, closer."

Shu squared his shoulders and crossed to the Iaen. Its intimidating height and size were brought into sharp focus. Shu glanced back at Tor and, for a moment, it seemed that he was asking for a way out of this. Tor felt a momentary pang of guilt.

"I'm ready." Shu's voice was tremulous now. All the certainty of his faith had dissipated.

"Trust me."

Reluctantly, he complied, suddenly ashen and sheened with sweat.

Tor swallowed, nervous and agitated. The swirls of movement in the walls took his eye.

The Iaen paused for a moment then with a sudden, oddly balletic movement, drove its immense fist into the side of Shu's skull. His head snapped sideways and round. There was a sharp crack. Blood sprayed outwards from the impact point. He crumpled to the floor heavily and lay motionless at the Iaen's feet, his eyes wide, his head at a grotesque angle and resting in an expanding pool of blood.

Tor stumbled back. His stomach heaved. Farah was convulsed by loud, helpless sobs. Sergeant Olsen was screaming orders into her comm as she rushed forward, making for Shu's body.

The Iaen stepped into her path.

"Trust," it said then turned back to Shu, reached down and grabbed one of his arms.

"Stop," Sergeant Olsen yelled. Her sidearm was drawn, gripped now in both hands and aimed at the Iaen. "Release him and back away. *Now.*" She looked to be close to breaking point. She looked dangerous.

"Sergeant," Tor called to her. "Put down the weapon. Sergeant!"

She glanced at him, her expression one of confusion. This place had eaten into her professional confidence and reduced her to a shaking, pin-removed grenade.

The Iaen ignored the uproar and dragged Shu

unceremoniously to the wall. Once there, it hooked its hands under the Advisor's armpits and jerked him to his feet. For a moment, he stood in the Iaen's arms like a partner in a grotesque dance. His head flopped sickeningly onto his right shoulder. Then the Iaen pushed him against the wall.

The shadows within became increasingly energised, frantic almost. The Iaen held its burden in place, pressed against the translucent surface.

Sergeant Olsen faltered. She lowered her weapon. Silence fell. Everyone watched. Everyone was frozen in place, Tor on his feet, Farah beside him, muttering under her breath, her face tear-streaked.

For a moment, Shu's body appeared to sink into the soft fabric of the wall. Then he trembled, once. His head snapped back into place. He uttered a grunt then cried out in what sounded like raw agony. The Iaen released him and he staggered forwards. He clutched at his head. His mouth opened and closed as if he was trying to speak. No sound came at first. Tor was oddly unsurprised to see that he no longer bled and that his skull was uninjured. Shu brought his fist up to eye level and gazed in something resembling wonder as he opened and closed his hand. A beatific smile brightened his face. He spoke, a single, jarring word.

"Miracle."

*

The room was white, one of its walls broken by a huge arched window. The window was open. A breeze billowed the delicate drapes that hung there and gave glimpses of a huge moon that splashed silver onto the night-dark.

She was in a bed made luxurious by white satin.

She was not alone.

Katherina struggled to remember how she came to be here. Panicked, she rolled over to see Tor.

She was in his arms. She felt him. She smelled that

familiar meld of scents, aftershave, soap, a hint of alcohol, an undertow of sweat. She smelled his maleness, indefinable yet as much part of him as the spirals and twists of his DNA.

Katherina closed her eyes and let him crush her to himself. She felt the warmth of his flesh and of the bed.

"Where are we?" she asked.

"Here," his voice. It was *his* voice. The ambiguity of his answer was oddly comforting. Place didn't matter as long as *he* was there.

She rolled onto her back. Tor held her hand.

"Is this good?" he said.

"Yes, it's good."

"I miss this. I miss this with all my heart."

"So do I."

"I have to talk to you. I have to tell you something, about the Tal."

She waited and was troubled. This was wrong. She couldn't be here with Tor. That was over and done with. She was…She was confused, unable to recall where she was supposed to be.

"This is their planet, Katherina. This is *their* world."

How did he know that?

"No, this is Ia. This planet belongs to the Iaens."

"The Iaens are an invader. They are parasites who infest the Tal mind-homes and cause them to wither and die."

Mind-homes, the phrase conjured a startlingly vivid image of the huge structures that formed the city.

"But the Iaens are our allies."

"They have perpetrated genocide."

"I don't understand. That can't be true. The Iaens are good.

"They are neither good nor evil. They simply *are* in the way a virus or bacteria *is* and nothing more."

Tor slid his arm about her and drew her close again. She lay on his chest, comforted by its steady rise and fall. The feeling was good. He nuzzled her hair. She closed her eyes and he kissed her.

The kiss was long and deep. It sent her tumbling into darkness. The kiss was a spiralling, dizzying rush between stars and through the hearts of nebulae. The kiss consumed her then filled her and dissolved her until she was senses-only, untethered and drifting over forests, a storm darkened sea, a range of ice-blue mountains. Until –

There was a city.

Formed of countless pebble-like mind-homes that stretched towards and beyond the horizon. She felt the thrum of life that pulsed within each one. She was part of it. It was joyous. She reached out with her hands and they melted and flowed through the strands of the Tal thought-web. It was vast, mile upon mile of it, filled with infinitely complex weave of the one-mind. She dissolved in an electric waterfall of sensation and merged with the rush and noise and joy as she spiralled through strand after strand of the web. It stretched across the entire surface of the planet and then reached out into space and far beyond.

She felt herself lifted, into the sky, higher and higher until she could feel the hiss and throb of stars and the songs of gravity, quasars and black holes. And among it all, punctuating the glorious choir of the universe, she heard the chatter of uncountable civilisations.

Minds touched.

Thoughts, ideas, wisdom were shared.

There were those who thought the touch of the Tal to be the touch of God.

Then the Iaens came. A deafening signal, a hurricane of confusion and terror. They pierced the web and stormed through its threads and followed it straight to the heart of the Tal. They were formless and yet quickly moulded themselves into a rough-hewn imitation of their host.

Katherina felt them course through her. Felt them hack and hew and distort until she was rebuilt in their image. Felt them devour her from within.

She felt the exquisite pain of self-mutilation as the Tal severed the infected limbs from their one-structure to protect what was left of their *self*. Diminished and bleeding the Tal retreated and sought to heal. The Iaens were shut out, unable to make further gains. An uneasy stalemate descended.

Until now.

The Iaens had found an ally to complete their conquest. An ally whose hands it bloodied on their behalf. An ally who would let them in and willingly act as hosts in exchange for gifts that were dangled before them like toys offered to a child in order to bribe it into obedience –

There was light.

Katherina cried out and struggled to draw breath. She couldn't move. She was buried. She was suffocating. She opened her eyes, prepared to fight against the organic shroud that encased her.

And found herself free of it and lying on the floor in the chamber at the heart of the Tal mind-home.

Tor?

Katherina sat up and looked wildly around. She called out his name then realised that it had been an illusion, a dream, some hallucination that enabled the Tal to speak to her. Despite the realisation, she felt the wrench of loss.

She bit down on her hurt and forced herself to check the micro-comm. It was intact, thank God, and secure in its breast pocket outlet. Exhausted but needing to take some sort of action, she hauled herself to her feet.

"I want to help," she called out to the seemingly oblivious Tal who filled the chamber. "I've seen war. I know what it is." She stared at the embryo blisters on the wall. The Tal army was limitless. The humans could never win, but a lot of marines would die trying. The knowledge broke her heart. The common soldier was once again the weapon in the blood-soaked hand of the politician. "If you let me go back to my people, I'll do what I can to stop this –"

She didn't finish because she was knocked off her feet by an explosion.

*

The world was suddenly filled with smoke. She heard the

relentless hammer of automatic weapons. Stunned and half-deafened by the blast, Katherina became aware that she was on her knees, a dangerous place to be while bullets snapped about her. Bullets were dangerous. Deadly. She could be hit. She needed to do something.

A figure lurched out of the smoke. Big, indistinct, familiar. She struggled to remember what it was and where she was and what had happened. The figure stood over her for a moment, then crumpled and fell.

A marine.

No, its face was only half-formed, sketchy. A Tal version then.

It bled fluid and even as she watched began to sink and dissolve into the floor.

The Tal structure was burning. The stink was that of burning flesh. She knew that smell. She had breathed that smell as a marine. The stench of it twisted her gut and she vomited.

Bullets.

Christ.

She threw herself forwards, cheek pressed hard against the floor and prayed it wouldn't mistake her for a casualty and absorb her. Boots crashed by her. The shooting rose to a crescendo. Another body fell. It was a real marine this time. She lay on her side, eyes wide open, the only part of her that Katherina could see – that familiar blank stare into eternity. The floor of the building was already claiming her. It did not seem to distinguish between friend or foe. All organic matter was grist for its mill.

More marines appeared and one of them, screaming and sobbing, tried to pull his comrade free of the floor's embrace. Too late. The body disappeared and the floor closed over the marine's face. Her would-be rescuer sobbed and swore and slammed at the floor with the butt of his rifle. Katherina said nothing. She offered no comfort. Any movement or sound would be seen as a threat. The marine was out of control. He would shoot first.

Everything was noise and heat and the stink of burning.

A cease fire order rang out. The shooting died down.

"Human here!" Katherina shouted in response. "Civilian!"

"Stay down, I repeat stay down while we locate you."

Katherina did as she was told. The marines would be slow and cautious in case this was a ruse. They would also be trigger-happy.

Katherina started as a rifle muzzle was jabbed into her back.

"Human found."

"I'm Katherina Molale, a member of the journo pack with Secretary Danielson's delegation." Her voice sounded distant in her own ears, muffled, disconnected.

"ID?"

"Left pocket of my overall."

She tried not to flinch as a hand slid into her pocket. She felt her journo pass being removed. She remembered the micro-comm. The device would be immediately confiscated if the marine found it. A moment. Then. "Okay, you can get up now, Ms Molale."

She did so, slowly, still shocked and disorientated by the suddenness of the assault. She coughed. The chamber was obscured by smoke. The bodies of the fallen were not visible and nor would they be. The building would have consumed all organic waste. Her ears rang. The marines were vague, shadowy shapes in the murk. She saw the grief-maddened marine, who had beaten the floor with his rifle, still on his knees and being comforted by a comrade. There was a hand on his shoulder. He sobbed.

"Belyaev, hey Belyaev, pull yourself together." The marine's comforter was an officer, a lieutenant. Katherina recognised the sleeve flashes.

The marine, Belyaev, nodded and after a moment was helped to his feet by a couple of his buddies.

"Okay?" the lieutenant asked him.

"Yeah, yeah, I guess so." He didn't sound okay.

"I want you to escort Miss Molale back to the command unit, then get yourself some coffee and some rest. Got that?"

"Yes sir."

The lieutenant turned away and called out a new order. "The rest of you, let's fry us some eggs."

Katherina saw the grey ghosts that were the marines move into the smoke. They were, she realised, making for the walls and the blisters that held the Tal embryos.

"Can you walk?" Belyaev's voice was hoarse from his outburst of grief and he didn't sound young. He was anonymous in his uniform and body armour. His face was hidden by a helmet and visor.

"I'm okay, I'm not injured," Katherina said. She wavered dizzily. The faintness passed.

"Did they hurt you?"

"What?"

"The Tal, did they torture you?"

"I was treated well." Dragged here by her arm, ignored, buried alive. Yet…

She sensed Belyaev's surprise. He turned away and set-off into the smoke without a further word. Katherina didn't catch up with him until they were in the tunnel that formed the entrance to the building. As she did so, she heard the liquid roar of flamethrowers. Eggs were being fried.

"I didn't think they took prisoners," Belyaev didn't look round when he spoke. His voice was a shout, barely heard above the noise of the flamethrowers. "I thought they shot you whether you were shooting back or had your hands in the air."

"Well, for whatever reason, they chose not to shoot me," Katherina shouted back. "I need to speak to your commanding officer. I found something out while I was in there. They told me who they were, what this war is about." Why was she telling this guy, a grunt, someone here to obey orders and not think too much? "Look, I'm a little shaken, I've said too much. And this isn't simple. The Tal are not…" She gave up. "Have you got any water?"

Belyaev finally stopped and turned round. He handed her a flask from his utility belt.

"Thanks."

"How long have you been here, ma'am?"

"A few hours, I think. I'm not sure. My name's Katherina, by the way."

"Nice name," Belyaev said.

"Thanks. How long have *you* been here?"

"Too long," There was an undertone in Belyaev's voice. Regret? Unease? "I heard you mention a delegation. Are there peace talks? Is there going to be a cease fire?"

"I don't know. I'm a journo. I'm sorry." The regret she put into her voice wasn't entirely faked. She felt that it might be a good idea to get Belyaev on her side. "I understand how you feel. I know what it's like to be in the middle of something like this."

"Oh yes?" Belyaev's scepticism sounded out of character. "And how would *you* know what it's like 'to be in the middle of something like this?' With all due respect, making news vids isn't the same as being in the firing line."

"I was a marine."

"Which unit?" Still sceptical.

"The 14th. I fought in the Antarctic campaign."

"A Hellbringer? You were a Hellbringer?"

Sighing, Katherina rolled up her sleeve for the second time since she had arrived on this planet to reveal the tattoo. There was a long moment, then Belyaev extended his gloved hand.

"An honour, ma'am."

"Katherina."

His hand closed about hers and his grip was firm. The contact was pleasant. Katherina experienced a startling pang of regret when the handshake ended.

"Not many of you survived," Belyaev said.

"I lost a lot of friends." All her friends. "But then, you know what that's like." Katherina felt the old emotion uncoil. She fought it down. It was the past. It was done. Except it wasn't done was it? Because here they were again, humans engaged in killing and destroying once more. And, as always, on the shakiest of moral grounds.

Belyaev shrugged, but the gesture was an act; the soldier's fake resignation, used to cover deep, bitter grief. "We're taking losses. We can't seem to finish this. The more Tal we kill, the more of them there are. How the hell are we supposed to beat a horde of aliens who can come back from the dead?" They reached the entrance and stepped outside. Katherina was shocked to see that it was daylight. She had been in the Tal hive for most of the night and yet it had felt like only moments. Men and equipment were pouring into this and other adjacent buildings and taking up positions around their bases.

"And how the hell are we supposed to kill our own, and women and kids."

"They're not real," Katherina said.

Belyaev pushed up his visor and breathed deep. His face was heavily lined, his eyes pools of blackness. He uttered a rueful, humourless chuckle. "They look fucking real when you have them in your sights." He shook his head and sighed. "I don't understand why we don't just tight-nuke the whole area and be done with it. We have a shipload of missiles over our heads." He waved towards the fire-blanked sky and set off walking again.

"A shipload?"

"Yes, there is a cruiser up there. How the hell do you think we got here?" He stopped walking again. "Didn't you know about that?"

How to answer. She paused for a beat then came to a decision. "No, Belyaev, I didn't know. No one knows. As far as everyone is concerned, we're negotiating some form of limited military aid for the Iaens. This war is a secret war."

"I go where I'm sent and I do as I'm told, ma'am." Belyaev was suddenly distant and sullen. The ma'am was no slip of the tongue. Katherina resigned herself to a new friendship, quickly lost. And it had felt like friendship, not the false camaraderie with Private Nakamura she had conjured-up to get off the lander.

"Of course. I'm sorry," Katherina said. "I should have kept my mouth shut."

They walked on through a smoke-misted landscape of destruction. Hanging over it was a cloying meld of burning, and dead-flesh scents. Katherina and Belyaev met marine armour and troops, moving forward into new positions somewhere deeper in the city. The marines must have launched a counterattack last night, driven the Tal assault back, burned more buildings and taken new ground.

"You're saying that this war is illegal?" Belyaev said suddenly. They were walking, side-by-side now. Katherina was having trouble with the stench. She felt the urge to vomit. It felt as if she was walking through Hell and trying to make conversation with one of the demons who dwelt there.

"According to Alliance rules, it is," she said.

"I don't understand." He didn't look at her when he spoke.

"We have to stop fighting them. We have to stop this war."

"We?" His laughter dripped cynicism. "So, how are *we* going to do that?"

"I have to get back to the other side of the barrier. Once there..." She could send the micro-comm footage to the Alliance, but the consequences of that would be devastating for humanity. Probably banishment for Earth, plus the crippling economic and social effects such a punishment would bring in its wake. No, she needed to talk to Tor.

Belyaev didn't need to know that. He was a good soldier. He did his duty, which meant that he might not be able to go against his instincts and loyalties. "I have a way in to the Chief Secretary. I can talk to him."

"I'm taking you to the command crawler. They can get you back."

She doubted it. Whoever was in charge here would see her as a security risk. She would be detained and possibly shot if circumstances demanded it.

"No. I need to get back to the lander –"

A salvo of the rockets slammed into an armoured

crawler about fifty metres from where Katherina stood. The impact was deafening. Flame erupted and burning debris was hurled high into the air. She hit the ground as gravity slammed the wreckage Ia-wards in a deadly shower of hot metal. A moment later, she heard more rockets streak overhead. Bullets snapped.

"Breakthrough!" someone yelled.

Katherina lifted her head to see marines snap into action around her. They pounded down the street to staunch the bleed. Half-crouched, hands over her ears, Katherina looked up to see Belyaev. His head was bare, helmet dropped to the ground beside his boots. His face was blank, his eyes as expressionless as those of the Tal. His lips moved, but whatever words he spoke were stolen by the din. A tear tracked its way through the grime on his stubbled cheek.

Katherina tried to clear the fury and blood-roar from her head. She had to get up. This was her chance to get out of here. She wanted to help Belyaev but how could she? The only way was to get back to the lander and expose this lie. She struggled to her feet and barged through a platoon of oncoming troops and out into the smouldering ruins beyond the marine lines.

Behind her, the noise of conflict grew loud. She stumbled to a halt, out of breath, too exhausted to run any further. She trembled. Shock perhaps. She had to keep going. She had to force herself into a run. Smoke provided a thin veil over the destruction in which she stood. Bodies were strewn across the streets between the torn hulks that had been Tal buildings. There was no time to clear up, no time for decent burial. Suddenly she wanted to get away, but escape seemed impossible.

Hatch open, ramp down. Out, come on, out, out, out!

The bodies hemmed her in. Explosions shuddered through the ground and drove upwards into her belly. The crack of small arms jangled on her nerves. She was dizzy, blood rang in her ears and in her head. She couldn't move.

Marines crumpled and fell, bleeding, into the freezing

surf. Others made it onto the ice and shingle before their flesh and bones were punched out of their bodies by machine-gun bullets or their limbs were torn-off by mortar shells.

She wanted it to stop. She wanted to scream.

*

A miracle.

And it was.

Tor stood in the plaza, a few steps from the lander's ramp and the watching eyes of the marines that guarded it. He was alone. He needed the film of Shu's murder and resurrection to stop running through his brain. The babbling, shock-fuelled excitement of the delegation, the arguments, demands and shouting only served to make the thing run through his skull faster and faster until he couldn't fucking *think*.

A miracle.

Except, it wasn't. There was nothing supernatural about this. Shu's apparent return from the dead was a bio-chemical process, so advanced that to his own Neolithic mind, it was magic. But it was not divine intervention and it wasn't a miracle.

He also knew, however, that to Shu it was. Tor had seen the adoration on his face as he became aware of what had happened to him and had known, in that instant, that the negotiation was lost.

It had been several minutes after the *miracle* when Tor had finally managed to speak. His question was inevitable. "What else are you capable of?"

"The repair of all organic material," the Iaen answered.

Tor hesitated, frightened by the enormity, and inevitability, of his next question. "Does that include disease?"

Cancer?

"Yes."

"Immortality."

"Yes."

"And you're offering this to humankind?"

"Yes." The gift would come with a price, of course. "In return for full military assistance in our conflict with the Tal?"

Tor closed his eyes for a moment then gathered his wits together and returned to the lander.

*

Farah spoke first. "This is cruel."

Everyone appeared to have calmed down. The delegation was crowded, once more, into the coffin-sized hold-come-conference room

"Cruel?" Shu asked. "How can you –"

Farah ignored him "Mr Secretary, this is crass, emotional blackmail."

"Look at me." Shu was on his feet. "I was dead and now I am alive. How can we turn our backs on a gift as wonderful as this?"

"The President must have known about this." Tor leaned across the table towards his chief advisor. "Did *you* know?"

"Of course I didn't know –"

"Don't lie to me. I'm sick of lies. The Iaens are lying. You're lying. The President lied."

"Be careful, sir." Farah this time.

"Yes, yes, you're right, Farah. I have no proof." Tor looked at Lisa. "What about you? Did you know?"

She shook her head. "Of course I didn't."

"But you did, didn't you, Shu."

"You're treading on dangerous ground, Mr Secretary. I respectfully request that you retract your accusation."

"What else do you know? Do you have information on the Tal? On this so-called war?"

"Mr Secretary, up to now, this whole mission has been a failure. You have no agreement. You have made no progress. Your strategy seems to be to antagonise the Iaens –"

"You want it to fail, don't you. You want military

intervention because you want what the Iaens are offering to us. To me."

Ever the peacemaker, Farah tried to intervene. "Mr Secretary, I really feel —"

"It's all right Farah. It has to be said. I've been set-up. Why? Because the promise of a cure for my daughter would be too much for me to resist. Who can turn their back on the promise of everlasting life, brought to you courtesy of the Iaens."

"Sir —" Shu was on his feet.

Tor rose to face him. He was losing control, but he didn't care. "People will pay any price for this. People will willingly sell their freedom in exchange for eternity. What's democracy and free speech and freedom of belief in comparison with that? God help us, Shu, you'll probably be seen as the new messiah, martyred then risen from the grave to bring healing on your wings. I will not be blackmailed. I will not be bribed into making a decision that will end with humankind being thrown out of the Alliance and transformed into a galactic pariah."

"We wouldn't need the Alliance," Shu replied quietly.

"What?"

"If the Iaens bestow this gift upon us, humankind would be immortal. No more disease, no aging. We would have all the time we need to expand through the galaxy, to build our own alliances, on our own terms."

"I should have known," Tor said wearily. "You're a Separatist."

"I have no agenda. Mr Secretary, you should want what is best for your daughter?"

The last vestiges of Tor's self-control shattered. He lunged at Shu and managed to grab a fistful of his tunic before Lisa and Farah had his arms and dragged him back. For a moment, frustration fired him into an angry struggle, then, he felt his strength fail and he let them guide him back into his seat.

Shu remained on his feet, flushed, but recovering quickly. He managed to exude outrage mingled with pity.

"That was…That was most unseemly, Mr Secretary. I

believe an apology is in order."

"And I believe you should get out," Farah said. "Before I finish what Secretary Danielson started."

Shu made to retort then obviously thought better of it and left.

Tor rested his head on the back of his chair and closed his eyes. "Thank you, Farah." God, he was tired. "I'm sorry. If any of you want to distance yourself from me then I would understand. No point your careers being washed into the same sewer as mine."

"I have no reason to walk away," Farah said.

"You'll never be rid of me," Lisa Kavanagh said.

Tor didn't trust himself to speak at that moment. Farah pressed a mug of coffee into his hand. It was foul-tasting, but welcome.

"I need to talk to the President," Tor said.

*

Now alone in the conference room and waiting for the link to be established, Tor experienced a sudden and painfully vivid memory of Eva's first breath and first cry. He remembered the wonder of the curled, slippery thing that slithered into the doctor's hands. Dear God, how Eva had cried, minute fists clenched, miniature face screwed into a mask of fiery rage.

He remembered how he, a man utterly indifferent to children, had fallen in love with her the instant he saw her. He remembered how she had taken away his dignity and drawn him into her childish games. He had allowed her to plaster his features with face-paint. He had attended her tea parties and pretended to eat toy cakes and sipped imaginary tea from tiny plastic cups. He remembered how she had taken away his certainty and replaced it with fearfulness over her safety and her future. She had dissolved his ability to make rational judgements where she was concerned and turned him into an adoring fan of all her endeavours, no matter how infantile and unformed. She had delighted, entranced, enthralled, infuriated, enraged and then broken him and rebuilt him as someone more complete, more *human*.

Now, she was going to die. He was certain of it. The conviction stopped his breath and turned his mind to an electric scramble of panic and grief. He would let the grief flow, but this time, he must *not* let it mar his judgement.

Tor lay on his seat, now converted to a cramped and uncomfortable bunk, and covered his eyes with his arm. He needed to talk to the President, but he also needed to talk to Annika. He needed to see her. He needed to hear her, even if it was to listen to her cold-voiced recriminations. He needed to know what was happening. He needed to know if Eva was still alive.

Because, if she was, she could be brought here and healed in moments. All it would take was a simple "aye" and the Assembly would have their unanimous vote and the Iaens would have their war.

A knock. The door opened. Farah. "We have a link, sir."

*

Ten minutes later he was in the lander's control unit, seated at the deep-space comm. President Janaki Ammal's image appeared, painted with her usual warm smile. Tor found himself looking for deceit in her expression, but none was visible. She had hidden it away as only a politician could hide it.

"Secretary."

"Madam President."

Are you a Separatist? he wanted to ask her. Ready to dispense with the Alliance and let the human race – a heavily armed and unkillable human race – carve its way through the galaxy on its own terms?

"How are the negotiations, Tor?"

"Difficult. I'm still trying to establish the whereabouts and nature of the Tal."

"I understand."

"The Iaens claim that the Tal are a wider threat, to Earth and to the Alliance."

The President looked grave. "I was afraid of that."

"I have no way of verifying this. The Iaens are reluctant to show me any evidence."

"Of course, we need evidence, but surely the Iaens are not going to lie to us. Why else would they want us involved militarily?"

"I'm not sure."

A moment. Then, "And the gift they have for humanity?"

You know already.

"They can heal the sick and raise the dead."

They can heal Eva.

A moment, President Ammal's acting skills at their most formidable. "Heal the sick?" She closed her eyes and shook her head as if overwhelmed by emotion. She recovered and was matter-of-fact once more. "And the price?"

"Full military intervention."

"To destroy a potential threat to ourselves."

"That is the claim."

"You persist on calling it a claim, Tor."

"Yes, because, until proved otherwise to my satisfaction, that's what it is. I must know more about the Tal, overfly the battle zones. Anything."

"I knew I sent the right person for this, Tor. Many others would have capitulated when they saw what the Iaens have to offer. But even with your own tragedy unfolding, you persist in your battle for truth." And there it was. The edge, the grain of irritation. The impatience. Perceptible only to those who were looking for it. "You're a future president, Tor, make no mistake. Arrange a visit. Invoke my authority. You have the casting vote. I will stand by your decision."

Contact was broken. A moment then Annika appeared on the screen. There had been no improvement, but at the same time, no further deterioration in their daughter's condition. It was only a matter of time. He asked to see her. Then regretted it. She lay, ashen and still on the bed. Her hair was combed back from her face. There were dark smudges about her tightly closed eyes. She was connected to machines and drips. Tor was almost convinced that she had already gone and what he saw were her mortal remains, an empty shell, sustained by electricity and fluids.

Annika did not return to the screen. Contact was broken.

Tor was alone.

*

Katherina started as a hard object was jabbed into her side. She opened her eyes, rolled onto her back and peered up to see a marine. He seemed immense, a dark, anonymous shape, silhouetted against the sky. The rich blue behind him was dirtied by a trail of smoke. Too exhausted to move, Katherina waited for the order to get up and raise her hands. This then was the end.

"Katherina," the marine said and she realised that he wore no helmet.

"Belyaev? They sent you to deal with me?"

"They didn't send me anywhere." He crouched down and offered her a canteen.

Katherina sat up. Her body felt heavy and stiff. She drank. The water was cold and sweet in her throat.

"Thanks." She handed the canteen back. "What do you mean, *they didn't send you?*"

"I'm finished," he said. His voice held a tremor. "I was finished when Nina was killed."

Nina? Presumably the marine who had fallen beside Katherina in the Tal mind-house.

"Something's happened. There was an order. A fucked-up order." He sighed heavily, shook his head then continued. "We have to let some of the Tal through."

"Let them through?"

"All those people dead and now we have to let the bastards through."

Katherina was suddenly alert and awake. "Have you surrendered?"

"No. No one's surrendered. Maybe it's a tactic. I don't know. We have to let them get to the barrier. We have to let them break through into the Iaen city." He sighed again. "Whatever the reason, I no longer care. I'm finished."

*

"Sir." Farah was gently shaking Tor awake. "The Iaen is outside. It wants to talk to you."

Tor blinked and groaned. Whatever sleep he had been granted had done little to relieve his tiredness. He needed solitude, time to think and escape from the clamour of the debate. He wasn't going to get that until they returned to the *Kissinger*.

He had no doubt in his mind as to the decision he should make. He should vote against military action. He was a supporter of the Alliance. He believed in it and saw membership as the best course for the human race as it slowly fumbled its way across the galaxy. The Alliance was patient. It protected humankind both from the alien and, more importantly, from itself.

He had to vote against the motion.

And yet, tattered remnants of Mendelssohn's Violin Concerto clung to his befuddled thoughts as he struggled with the bleariness of sudden awakening from bad sleep. The dream image of Eva's ashen, near-corpse remained vivid and debilitating.

He knew his need to seek evidence of the conflict and his demand that contact be made with the Tal were disingenuous. He was playing for time, something that neither he nor Eva possessed in any great measure.

He hauled himself off the bunk and onto his feet. He quickly washed his face and dragged a comb through his hair then returned to the cabin where the rest of the delegation waited for the hatch to open. Tor asked Lisa if there was any news of Katherina. No point in faux formality. Ms Molale was Katherina to him and everyone in the delegation knew why.

"No sir. I'm sorry. A marine patrol was sent out into the city but found nothing. The truth is that we don't know where to look."

"You won't find her if she doesn't want to be found." Tor glanced round at the other members of the delegation, all of whom looked the worse for wear from lack of sleep.

The hatch opened. Outside it was warm but pleasant. The heat from the massive sun, still low in the cloudless sky, was countered by a cool breeze. There were mountains, visible in the spaces between the buildings, blued by distance.

The Iaen waited at the bottom of the ramp. Shu stood next to it.

"What are you doing?" Tor demanded. "What the hell is going on?"

"I have taken matters into my own hands." Shu said. "You'll be pleased to learn that I have persuaded the Iaens to grant us access to the battlefield."

You bastard, Tor told him silently. He knew he was beaten. How could he rebuke the man for achieving what he, himself, had been unable to.

"Good work." The words tasted foul in his mouth.

"I cannot vouch for your safety" said the Iaen.

"You should take the lander," Shu said. "The Iaens have told me that you can overfly the conflict zone."

Told *you*? Tor bit down on his resentment.

"Shall I order the pilot to prepare for flight, sir" Farah said. "It could take a while to get the craft air-ready."

"Yes," Tor answered. "The sooner we do this the better."

"With your permission, Mr Secretary," Shu said. Since when did he need my permission? Tor thought bitterly. "I would like to stay here with the Iaens. We have begun a fascinating discussion on the nature of God, and the very definition of the Divine."

"Of course," Tor said. If he was honest with himself, he

was relieved to be rid of the man for a few hours. He had changed since his resurrection or was it that Tor's view of him been altered by the impossibility of his being alive.

*

And this time, she played beautifully. Tor sat back and drank it in. He felt Annika's hand close about his and let the tears come, unashamedly. That was his daughter over there, behind the music-stand in their private lounge, conjuring beauty from her violin. Even the movement of her arm as she drew the bow over the instrument's strings was graceful. The change had been sudden. So little time passed between the awful screeches and howls produced when she was a child, to this.

He let the music seep into him. He didn't close his eyes though. He needed to watch. He needed to remember this moment because the poignancy of the music only served to emphasise the poignancy of their lives. She was ill. She was pale and thin and her time was short, unless some cure could be found that actually worked.

So little time. What did that mean? Why was he feeling so near to breaking down? The music slid through him and wound itself about his heart. He drew his wife to him and held her. Through his veil of tears he watched that slim, elegant daughter of theirs play and let the music pierce him.

Wrong. This was wrong.

Something was wrong, with her arms. Blotches had appeared, darkening to black, expanding, crawling over her fair skin. On her face, too. She was oblivious. Her eyes closed as she played. The blotches were the colour of bruises. They expanded and joined until her arms were black with them. They blossomed from her neck and up over her face.

The music faltered and became discordant. It was a terrible cry of pain, perfect and clear. A cry of despair. Her hair fell over her face, she hunched, collapsed.

Annika was angry. She slapped him and ripped Tor's

cheek with her nails and screamed at him that this was his fault. His fault. His fault.

As his daughter crumpled to black, swirling dust –

Tor woke with a cry of fear. He jerked forward in the seat and tried to slow his breathing. He was damp with sweat. The music still rang in his head. He realised that Farah was leaning over him.

"Comm link, sir. Personal channel."

Tor struggled to his feet and followed her to the control cabin.

Annika.

She was ashen, her eyes dark from crying and lack of sleep. "How much longer? You need to come home. We're losing her. Damn it, Tor, come home."

"Annika...slow down, please. I've just woken up."

"I don't care. You have...to...you have to come home. Oh Tor..." She broke down. She doubled-up and sobbed and it was as if the last ounce of her will were flowing from her as tears.

"I will as soon as I can. I'll come home Anna."

Yes, he would. He was giving in. He couldn't take any more of this. He had to get back to Earth and he had to help Eva in the only way possible.

"They knew about our daughter. How could they do that to us?" Annika's anger was wrought with grief. She sobbed as she shouted at him.

That's why *they sent me, Anna, because they knew...*

"Tor! Tor, are you listening?"

"Yes, I am. Anna, I will come home. Tell them to keep her alive. Please, make no decisions until I return."

*

Katherina followed Belyaev along the streets between the ruined structures that she no longer saw as buildings. They were re-growing. She saw clean walls, emerging from the blackened fire wreckage. Humankind could never defeat the Tal through conventional warfare. Belyaev had been right, only a tight-nuke barrage would put an end to the Tal. They and everything connected to them was indestructible. You couldn't defeat immortals.

And why should they? This was the Tal home world. This did not belong to the Iaens and it was no business of humankind to interfere.

She and Belyaev had been walking for an hour or so. They had put distance between themselves and the front line. There were no obviously human reserve positions, no dressing stations, nothing but ruin.

They could hear the conflict, however, bursts of gunfire, explosions made dull and heavy by distance. Katherina was appalled by what Belyaev had told her. Countless lives had been sacrificed and now, at the whim of some politician, the surviving marines had been ordered to give way.

A sudden skirmish broke out close by.

Streams of tracer arced out towards her. Katherina stayed low, praying that she could avoid stray bullets. It would only take one. Or an explosion. A grenade. Her own residual fighting instincts drove her to the ground. The shockwave hit. She felt her already battered eardrums bend painfully. Dust and debris. A prolonged burst of fire. Both sides were taking heavy punishment. This was building towards a major offensive.

Then the noise of firing lessened. She sensed a sudden pocket of silence away to her right.

"I have to take a look." Katherina had no choice. She was a journo. She always chased the story.

Belyaev made to protest but Katherina was already on the move.

There was no further shooting here. No grenades or rockets, no screams or yelled orders. There was that eerie quiet, a bubble of silence bordered by the rest of the war. A cool breeze slowly tugged the smoke apart to reveal Tal fake marines winding through the ruin like running water that divided and re-formed about rocks in the stream. They had a strange grace about them. A lightness of foot that was far from human.

She followed them, a hundred yards to their right,

keeping low. Ahead, she saw more burning buildings and ruined equipment, but no sign of the defenders, except for their dead. The air was tainted with oily smoke. Ahead, the scenery shimmered, as if it was reflected in water. She realised that it was a reflection. The barrier was ahead and the Tal were passing through it into the Iaen-controlled part of the city.

*

"We go." An Iaen had emerged from the lander's cockpit. It was identical to the negotiator, but seeing as Shu hadn't returned, Tor could only assume that this was a different individual, although there was no telling what the truth was when it came to both the Iaens and the man who had been his chief advisor.

And did the word individual even apply to the Iaens?

Farah was strapped-in. Lisa had just returned from briefing the journo pack, all of whom had decided to come along. Too big for a seat, the Iaen sat on the floor in the aisle. Pre-flight checks must have already been completed because no sooner were the hatches sealed than the engines erupted into life and the craft lifted queasily from the ground.

Flying always made Tor glad he had not indulged in a heavy breakfast. He turned his attention away from the porthole, but not in time to miss the city cant dizzyingly as the flyer went into a tight turn and set-off southwards. The pilot held the craft's speed down. A low altitude was called for so that the delegation could best observe the conflict. This meant that the craft was forced to plot a zig-zag course through the Iaen buildings. None of it was conducive to pleasant flying.

A shape caught Tor's attention. He peered out of the port and saw a second flyer, painted drab marine olive and bearing their insignia on its flank. Where the hell had that come from? There had to be a cruiser somewhere nearby, probably in orbit. No one had told him about that. This was serious. Cruisers were immense, heavily armed and capable of carrying an entire army with all their equipment, and launching a fast strike should his vote be for military action

Why hadn't he been told?

The rough air buffeted the vessel.

"Secretary." It was the Iaen.

"Yes? What?" Rude and abrupt, but he no longer cared.

"We are approaching the conflict –"

The timing was so horribly perfect it was almost a bad joke.

Because that was the moment the lander was hit.

Time slowed. Reality splintered. There was noise first, a loud bang followed by a crunch as if metal was being screwed into a ball by a giant fist. The rear of the craft was kicked up, forcing the nose downwards and it felt as though the lander had come to a sudden, violent halt in the sky. Tor was rammed forward against his belt. Both Farah and the Iaen were snatched away and thrown towards the lander's nose. Then came the shockwave, heat and smoke that stung Tor's eyes and scratched at his throat. He coughed and gagged, fearing that its toxicity would kill him if the crash didn't.

The descent changed from a shallow dive to a corkscrew. The world spun. The city and the sky blurred into a sickening grey madness. Tor was jammed against the outer hull, his belt dug into him so tight he could barely breathe. They were going to crash, to die. He felt an odd resignation sweep through him. Any moment now it would be over. Done. Gone. The engines screamed.

A sudden lurch then the spinning stopped. The lander skidded round and every cell in Tor's body vibrated as the landing jets ignited. He could see nothing through the thickening smoke. He could barely breathe, the temperature was rising towards unbearable. He could feel, rather than see the flames behind him as the rear of the lander burned.

They descended, slowly. Why didn't the pilot hurry? They had to get out. They had to land. There was fuel and there was fire.

One of the landing jets cut out. There was another explosion, below the floor, an oddly distant, muted blast that seemed to have little to do with what was happening. The lander tipped to the right.

Then hit the ground.

Tor's jaws were slammed tighter. His teeth clashed and he felt as if every vertebra in his spine was jammed against its neighbour. The surviving landing jets cut. There was shouting. Tor saw Farah emerge from the smoke. Her clothes were torn. She was bleeding from a cut lip, and from a gash in her forehead. Someone was screaming.

Farah slammed the heel of her hand into the buckle of Tor's belt then grabbed at the front of his overall and yelled into his face to get up, get up, get up, *get up.*

Tor hauled himself across the seats and into the aisle, then fell against the opposite seats. People shouted and screamed. The hatch was open and smoke was pouring in. He glanced back and saw flames lick through an immense tear in the rear bulkhead. Something that resembled a charred mannequin was slumped in its burning seat.

The journos were in there. Lisa. Oh Christ, Lisa had been sitting in that seat.

He crawled, trying to hold his breath. Hands were on him, hauling him up the short but unclimbable hill that was the aisle. He scrabbled with his feet. He coughed, barely able to breathe now. The hands belonged to a marine, and to Farah. He was at the hatch, then out onto the ramp, which was buckled and wrong, but his salvation.

He kept his eye on the back of the person who appeared in front of him in the swirling, all-but impenetrable smoke. A journo. The man was coughing, bent double. Tor staggered forwards, momentarily blinded then out into the light and air.

Others were already here.

Tor dropped to his knees and sucked in a lungful of the air. He felt a hand on his shoulder. Farah.

"Secretary, are you okay?"

"In a better state than you, by the look of it."

"A handful of the journos made it out, don't know about the crew or the Iaen.

"The marines?"

"Some survived, but half of them were in the rear cabin, where the rocket hit…"

"Rocket?"

"Yes sir."

"We were shot down?

"Yes –"

"Sir!" It sounded like a marine. A warning shout.

Tor, who was sitting on the ground now, trying to gather his scattered wits, looked up and saw figures emerge from the smoke near the lander.

Large, tall, familiar. As they came into the clear light, he saw that they were marines. Thank –

The nearest of them opened fire. From the hip. The marine who had issued the warning was wrenched up onto his toes, an absurdly balletic movement, then hurled back to the ground. One of the journos was hit next. His chest took three bullets which tore messily out of his back.

Shock froze Tor to the spot. It was wrong. They were making a mistake. They didn't realise who they were.

"The Tal!"

Tor looked up to see an Iaen emerge from the entrance to the nearest of the buildings.

"The Tal." Another from the adjacent structure.

"The Tal."

"The Tal."

From every building, a lone Iaen emerged and took two or three steps from the entrance and stood, declaring the enemy's name until they were struck down. Each time, another took its place. It was madness. A score, fifty, a hundred Ieans appearing in the entrances to their buildings and declaring the enemy over and over again. Their voices loud, echoing discordantly through the din of the skirmish.

The surviving marines had formed a loose defensive ring around Tor and were trying to hold back their fake counterparts. Tor struggled to understand. The Tal looked like human soldiers.

Whatever they were, there were too many. There were bodies on the ground.

There was blood. *Christ, blood.*

The lander's crew were crouched to his right, also using their sidearms. Several of the Tal had fallen, their bodies disturbingly human. There were countless reinforcements.

Tor heard the marine's sergeant shouting into her comm, asking for support and begging for suppressing fire. Tor's group moved back towards one of the buildings. A Tal broke free and ran towards Tor's party. It was disturbingly fast.

It stopped, as if frozen.

Another figure had run into its path. The figure was human, a woman. The Tal lowered its weapon and seemed unwilling to harm her. The strange incident was enough of a distraction for the humans to break for the building.

"Tor!" The woman shouted at him.

Katherina.

He watched her run, half-crouched, towards him. Tor saw two, three Tal emerge from the smoke in pursuit, though none of them raised its weapon to fire.

One of them fell.

The other two stumbled to a halt and, a moment later, were dissolved to bloody mist by a storm of cannon shells from the marine flyer that had provided escort to the lander. God bless that thing.

A Tal, armed with a rocket launcher, appeared. He swung the weapon upwards. The flyer swung round tightly and a burst from its forward turret slapped aside the threat in a single, bloody moment. The flyer dropped low, filling the world with its din. Dust and smoke were billowed outwards by its lander jets. Tor covered his eyes with his arm.

71

The jets roared again and the flyer raced skywards, leaving behind a company of marines, who fanned out across the street to engage with the Tal. Tor seized the moment to run to the building into which Katherina had disappeared.

He crashed to a halt inside the entrance, saw Katherina and a marine crouched against the wall. The marine was a grizzled, battle-hardened character who seemed to have lost his helmet.

Tor doubled-up, panting for breath. "What…What the hell is going on?" he gasped. "Where have you been?"

"You have to come with me." Katherina was on her feet, hand on Tor's arm.

"With you? Where?"

"You need to see it."

"Why didn't they attack you?" Tor asked. "Katherina, what's going on?"

"It doesn't matter. Not now. Please, just do as I ask."

"I can't do that. I can't simply walk away. I have people. Responsibilities. I have to report back…" Tor was suddenly too exhausted to talk anymore. He leaned against the wall and closed his eyes. The sound of the skirmish outside had diminished.

"Sir." The marine spoke this time. "The Tal were allowed to infiltrate this part of the city. We were ordered to let them through. It was a trap. It looks to me as if you were meant to be killed or injured."

"Or at least shaken up enough to make you vote for war," Katherina added.

"What are you talking about? Who allowed the Tal to break through?"

"What I found has changed everything," Katherina said. "Let me show you, Tor, please. We have to stop this."

"I don't understand –"

"For Christ's sake, Tor, I need you to see what's really happening here."

"I can't leave my people."

"Help will be on its way. There'll be more marine

flyers here in minutes and more ground troops. We're already fighting, don't you get it? Earth is already making war on the Tal."

*

Tor's home nation, along with most of Northern Europe, had escaped the worst of the water wars. They sent troops and aid and had been almost overwhelmed with refugees and beaten down by rationing, but no bomb had fallen, or bullet been fired within its borders. As a newly elected Council Member, Tor had been appointed Area Commissioner for Scandinavia. He had worked tirelessly to ensure that law and order were maintained, and that food and medical supplies were strictly controlled and distributed fairly. He barely slept for months. It had almost broken him, but he was noticed and his subsequent rise through the political ranks had been meteoric.

But through all his tribulation and triumph, he had never once stepped onto, or even seen, a battlefield.

More than fear, or even horror, it was dislocation that he experienced first. He had visited many alien worlds, witnessed the strange and the *wrong* many times, but this chaos, this devastated wilderness, was beyond anything he had ever seen. He could hear, taste and smell it. War was smoke and flame. It was a thunderous rumble, interspersed with the metallic chatter of small arms.

And there was the stench.

He knew immediately that it would be the stench that would follow him into his nightmares. It was sickly sweet, yet corrupt. It had made him vomit within minutes of his passing through the barrier and entering this place.

Tor saw charred and abandoned marine armour. He saw corpses, all of them human.

"The Tal buildings are re-growing," Katherina said.

Tor saw that the blackened flanks of the structures were peeling away to reveal clean new walls. The jagged wounds were meshed with a webbing of fibre on which new flesh grew.

"We can't win. My comrades are dying for nothing." The bare-headed marine, who had introduced himself as Belyaev, seemed to have assumed the role of minder. He was an angry and fearsome man, but Tor noticed that he was always gentle with Katherina.

The three of them moved deeper into the conflict zone. The marines they encountered were mostly silent and obviously exhausted. They sat or lay on the broken, debris-strewn ground, faces gaunt and expressions hollow.

Close to the front line, where talking became impossible above the roar and clatter of combat, the trio slumped down to rest in the lee of a wrecked land crawler. The machine listed to its left, the tracks on that side long gone. A huge hole was smashed into its flank. Tor didn't like to conjecture if its crew, or what was left of them, were still in there. He sat, arms over his knees, back against one of the crawler's wheels. He was out of breath. He was frightened and edgy. He was also thankful that Belyaev and Katherina's marine training had kept them safe so far.

So far.

Tor tried to shut his mind to the reality that it would only take one bullet, or one grenade and he would be snatched into whatever nothing it was that had taken the poor bastards strewn about him.

There was no God, he decided.

Home was suddenly bright in his mind. Annika, Eva, he wanted to get back to them more than anything else.

There was a way to save his daughter.

But there was also the Right Way. There was also the Alliance –

We don't need them, we can be immortal, we can transcend time, we could have the gift of forever

– and Earth's future.

Eva has no future.

"Tell me" he said to Katherina. "All of it."

She did, and he listened. She talked of stumbling into this place after seeing a marine flyer emerge from the barrier. She described her ordeal at the hands of the Tal. She described the vision. She described a war that was incomprehensible to humans, a war between two sets of communal souls.

"The Tal didn't try to kill me when I came for you Tor, because I seem to have some connection with them. They didn't harm me when they took me prisoner. They understood that I wasn't a soldier or their enemy. Perhaps they want me as a go-between." She shook her head, as if bemused. "Whatever it is, it's damned useful." She became serious again. "The Iaens promised us a gift, didn't they, Tor."

"There are two gifts, both of them equally as dangerous. The first grants the human race near-immortality –" *and I get Eva back from the dead.* "– the second, a god humankind can see and touch and talk to…"

Shu.

He wasn't on the lander. The bastard knew what was going to happen. So, who else had known? The President?

"Jesus, I'm everyone's patsy." Tor uttered a humourless, rueful chuckle. "They can't lose. If I'd been killed, they would have replaced me with a hawk guaranteed to vote with the rest of the Assembly, or the Iaens might have resurrected me from the dead. Who could experience that and vote against it? On the other hand, if I survived, which I have –"

So far.

"– they're counting on me being convinced that the Tal are the aggressor and that we have to intervene."

"We can stop this, Tor. I have it all here." Katherina held out her hand and Tor saw the micro-comm lugged into her palm. "Evidence we can to send to the Alliance. I was trying to get back to the lander to upload it. There's no chance of that now, but we can send it from the marines' command crawler."

"And they're going to let us do that?"

"I shouldn't need to, and I don't want to. It's too

damaging to Earth, but I will if it becomes necessary. You're the Chief Secretary. You outrank whoever is running this horror. Surely you can order them to stop."

She was right. If the Alliance knew what Earth was doing here, they would intervene immediately to put an end to hostilities. Their number included some terrifyingly advanced and powerful civilisations. They had ships and technology that would make the *Kissinger*, and that cruiser look like rowing boats manned by apes. Earth would not be treated well for their transgression.

"Okay, it's a plan. Belyaev, do you have any idea where the control crawler is?"

"I know where it *was*. They may have moved it back."

"Where it *was*, is a start."

*

How Belyaev managed to find navigation points and landmarks in this hell, Tor could not fathom. The marine led the way, crouched low but never hesitating. Tor followed, Katherina brought up the rear. She had slipped back into soldiering mode and it was hard to remember that she was a journalist and no longer a marine.

The din of battle grew louder with every step. The air was laden with its stink. The debris, the burnt skeletons of war machinery, the corpses strewn across the landscape with what looked like crazed abandon, ate into Tor's soul. A haze at once softened the landscape and transformed it into a monstrous graveyard in which the smoke-darkened silhouettes of ruined Tal mind-homes resembled the tombstones of giants.

But then wasn't that exactly what this place was? A cemetery? a charnel house?

Light flickered into the gloom. They were close enough to see muzzle flashes. Flame boiled upwards from the broken-tooth summit of a mind-home. A vehicle burned. Someone screamed. On and on it went, a relentless shriek for an end to whatever pain was being endured.

Now there were shouts, drowned by a series of

explosions that thudded into the ground like leviathan's footsteps. The shouting continued.

A dark shape loomed suddenly out of the murk. Blocky, bulky and solid. A little like a First World War tank to Tor's stinging, tired eyes.

Belyaev signalled Tor and Katherina to stay where they were then raised his hands, and cautiously approached the monster. A hatch opened. Light spilled out. There was a challenge. Belyaev shouted something back. The hatch slammed shut. The war crashed, rattled and thudded a hundred or so metres further on. Tor felt Katherina's hand close about his.

"Are you okay?" she said.

"Yeah, I think so."

He wanted to hold her and kiss her and take her back to himself.

He knew that he couldn't.

But for now, he held her hand and it was good. The contact was warm and seemed to expand outwards and through him to push his grief aside.

A larger hatch ground open in the crawler's flank, a ramp slid down. There, was once again, light, yellow-white and welcoming.

"Let's go," Belyaev shouted and ran towards the ramp.

Tor followed, still clutching Katherina's hand in his.

*

Colonel Grant was seated in the control chair, head-set in place, three-d goggles covering his eyes. The control room itself was bigger than Tor had imagined it would be. Dark though but starred by the constellations of pinprick lights that blinked and glowed from instrument panels on every wall. There was radio chatter, electronic beeps. Staff officers hurried in and out. There was urgency here, underlain with panic that was held in check by the solid presence of the commanding officer.

"Mr Secretary," he growled when he finally removed the goggles and scrambled to his feet. He sketched a weary salute, then added, "What the hell are you doing here, sir?"

"Might I ask you the same question, Colonel?" Tor had expected to feel anger when confronted with the man in charge here. Instead, he felt an instant and unexpected kinship. Grant was shouldering a burden just as he was and doing the best he could to bear it with the shreds of his honour intact.

"I'm following orders," Grant said.

The sinner's last resort, Tor mused.

"I have new orders for you, Colonel. Cease fire immediately."

"I can't do that, sir."

"And why not?"

"My orders are from higher up the chain."

"Higher?" There was only one person higher up in the chain of command than a Chief-Secretary "The President?"

"I'm sorry sir. Unless you have direct authority from the President, I cannot order a cease fire."

"Colonel, what happens if I agree to the Iaens' terms?" Tor said.

Katherina wrenched her hand free of his. "Tor –"

"I need to know. Colonel?"

"We immediately pull out of the war zone and let the *Sherman's* tight-nukes do the rest. The Iaens' barrier will protect the rest of the city from the blast."

Tor absorbed the information for a moment, then said; "Look at me. Do I look like a high-ranking official on a delicate diplomatic mission?"

"What do you mean?"

"I'm dirty, my clothes are torn and I'm bleeding, because the Tal were allowed through. They were probably supposed to kill me. Or, at least give the *Sherman* an excuse to send down more troops. Heightened tension. Escalation. How much do you know about that Colonel?"

Grant's lived-in face seemed to age before Tor's eyes.

"Orders again, is that it?" Tor said. "When the

President says let the Tal through, through they go."

"Sir, with all due respect –"

"We're talking about strings and puppets here and you know it," Tor said. "We're running out of time. Colonel, I can't countermand your orders. I understand that, but you do need to think carefully about this situation. Katherina, show him."

Katherina opened her right hand.

"A micro-comm ready to upload to the Alliance net. I have it all," she said.

Grant shook his head. He looked like a man close to breaking point. "You want me to disobey a direct order from the President. What is this, a coup d'état?"

"No," Tor said. "This is how you save Earth."

Grant stared at him for a long moment. "I want this to stop as much as you do," he said. "But there's only way it can stop, as far as I can see."

"There is another way." Tor's mouth was dry. Grant was right, this did amount to a coup. "Katherina is able to communicate with the Tal." An exaggeration perhaps, but a necessary one. "Order a ceasefire, Colonel, and she will confront them and ask them to stop fighting, at least until we can bring in the Alliance. They don't have to know about this dirty little war, but they need to be involved."

Grant turned his attention to Katherina. "Are you the journo who was captured? The one my troops found in that building?"

"Yes, sir. That's me."

"Can we trust her, Mr Secretary?"

"Yes, Colonel, you can. She has to do this," Tor said.

Grant appeared to consider the idea for several seconds. "I don't have any choice, do I, Ms Molale."

"Better an Alliance peace delegation than one of their battle fleets," Katherina said.

*

Tor watched Katherina leave and was suddenly alone. Belyaev was with her. Her loyal bodyguard and, potentially, a lot more judging by the chemistry between them. Tor felt a pang of jealousy. Ridiculous, because it was Annika he needed now. And Eva.

"Coffee, sir?" Grant said.

"Thanks."

Grant relayed the order to one of the staff officers who jumped to the task. A respected and feared officer, then, Tor observed. A good man trapped in a bad job.

"She's given us a way out," Tor said. The coffee arrived.

"Mr Secretary, we're throwing away one of the most wonderful gifts that mankind has ever been offered."

"You know about the Iaens' offer do you Colonel?"

"That's why I didn't resign when I was given this mission. I didn't want it, but…My wife died of cancer. If she could have lived a little longer…"

Cancer, that age old enemy of humankind and one that could be defeated at a stroke if he would only say "aye".

If she could have lived a little longer…

Tor felt an upsurge of grief. He was suddenly hot. His skin, clammy. His heartbeat fast and hard. It was difficult to breathe in here. Panic closed in about him. Suffocating, debilitating, raw panic.

What was he doing? He had a chance. Miracles were possible. The Iaens might be God, they might not be. It didn't matter. Humankind could fall at the Iaens' feet and worship them. He didn't care. None of that mattered now he held a miracle in his hand.

He held Eva's life in his hand

What the fuck was he doing?

The colonel's voice was steady, but his grief was clear in the bleak landscape of his face. "…I decided that this was a just war. We're protecting a race that is advanced and benign and unimaginably generous to humanity."

Oh yes, miracle-givers, that's what they are.

"You really saw it in such simplistic terms?" Tor didn't want to talk. He wanted Grant to shut up. He needed to think. He needed to clear his head.

I need a miracle.

"I should have known better. We were told that the Tal were little more than insects. That isn't what I found here. I don't really know *what* I've found here. But whatever it is, it's a different truth to the one I was sold."

Through the singing of his blood, Tor heard the plaintive cry of his daughter's violin. He saw her, clear in his mind, willowy and beautiful. His daughter. His love.

Christ, I need a fucking miracle.

"Get me a link to my wife and daughter please."

*

Out here, in the now-silent battlefield, Katherina felt the soft vulnerability of her human flesh more keenly than she had back in her marine days. There was little point in moving carefully. Belyaev was a few steps behind her. Katherina hoped the Tal would understand that he was her companion and, therefore, their ally. She held Tor's jacket as a flag and wondered if it was a futile gesture. The Tal would hardly recognise human surrender or truce signs, would they?

She walked through the ruined street. It was a place of corruption and death. She met columns of marines, pulling back from the front line. Grant had ordered a withdrawal to the second line defensive ring. The soldiers were grim-faced, tired and troubled. Many seemed relieved to see her and the columns parted willingly to let her through. It made her wonder if they had been told what she was going to do. She noticed that the sounds of firing had lessened. Did that mean that the Tal were content to allow the marines to retreat?

She reached a forward position where a handful of marines remained in place. There was no fighting.

"Why the hell don't they attack us?" one of them asked.

"Because we're not attacking them," Katherina answered. "You need to go."

"But ma'am –"

"Go," she said. "It's all right. They won't harm me."

The marines hesitated for a moment then crawled out

from behind their barricade and hurried away to catch up with their comrades. One of them told her to be careful. He sounded close to tears.

She steeled herself then stepped out into the no-man's land between the two front lines. She walked slowly over the cratered, smoking ground, until she was roughly halfway across then she stopped and waited. She sensed Belyaev's presence, always those few steps behind. She liked him. He was a good man.

Katherina prayed, although to whom she wasn't sure. She was surprised to discover that there was a part of her that did seem to know who God was and it was that part of her that mumbled incoherent pleas to the Divine.

A Tal stepped forward. A fake human marine, identical to, rough-hewn, crudely drawn but much larger than her former captor. Katherina walked up to the creature. It towered over her, an organic killing machine.

"I'm offering an end to your war with humankind. We never wanted war with your people, and I believe you never wanted war with us."

Silence. The Tal continued to stare at her. She pressed on, hoping it understood what she was telling it.

"I have evidence of this interference. It can be given to the Alliance in a moment. I don't want that to happen and I don't think it will. I believe that Colonel Grant is ready to withdraw from the conflict."

The Tal raised its organic rifle above its head. The weapon twisted in its hand then crumbled to dust. It turned and strode back to its lines. Others followed suit. Those weapons were for fighting humans only. Their struggle with the Iaens required only their minds.

Buildings burned, smoke billowed. Other than that, there was silence.

*

"I want to see her."

"Tor, there's nothing you can do."

"Annika, I want to see her. I need to see her. Please."

Annika stared at him from the screen for a few seconds. Her eyes were red and her gaze hollow. She sighed and turned away towards the room where Eva lay. A moment, then the vid-cam was switched to the critical care unit.

The control room was silent but for its electronic heartbeats and murmurings. Its pulse merged with the steady, artificial rhythm of Eva's life-support. Some remote, barely functioning part of Tor's awareness noted that the battle sounds outside had also stilled.

The cam focused in on his daughter. On her waxen complexion, on the umbilicals and wires that shuddered and trembled slightly as machines breathed and cleansed and pumped for her.

"Her hands. Show me her hands."

Annika didn't protest but moved the vid-comm down to where their daughter's beautiful left hand rested on the sheet. Tor studied her long, delicate fingers. Her wrist and the thin blue veins that threaded it. He saw that hand curled about the neck of her violin, fingers dancing on the strings as she drew the sweetest of musics from the instrument and from her soul.

A miracle, that's all she needed.

"Sir, comm coming in from Ms Molale."

"Put it through," Grant said. His own gaze was also fixed on the vid screen.

"Ceasefire agreed" she said. "I repeat, ceasefire will hold until Earth withdraws its forces. We just have to go home."

A miracle.

Katherina's voice was a distant thing. Without taking his eyes off his daughter, Chief Secretary Torstein Danielson heard himself give an order to Grant. Then he spoke to Katherina.

*

"I'm sorry."

"What? Tor, what are you saying?"

"Katherina, you have to get out. There are flyers on the

other side of the barrier. We're evacuating. They'll take you to safety. Hurry, there isn't much time."

"No, Tor, no, listen to me."

Silence. Comms cut. She couldn't move. She had to stay. She couldn't leave the Tal. Surely Marine Command wouldn't do this thing if they knew there was one of their own still out here. They never left one of their own behind.

She would stop this. Alone. Here.

No, not alone. She felt Belyaev's hand take hers.

When she was finally able to scream out her rage, the sound was lost in the roar of the incoming tight-nukes.

ENDS

Elsewhen Press
delivering outstanding new talents in speculative fiction

Visit the Elsewhen Press website at elsewhen.press for the latest information on all of our titles, authors and events; to read our blog; find out where to buy our books and ebooks; or to place an order.

Sign up for the Elsewhen Press InFlight Newsletter at elsewhen.press/newsletter

Gardens of Earth
Book I of The Sundering Chronicles

Mark Iles

Imagine an alien life force that knows your deepest fear, and can use that against you.

Corporate greed supported by incompetent surveyors leads to the colonisation of a distant world, ominously dubbed 'Halloween', that turns out not to be uninhabited after all. The aliens, soon called Spooks by military units deployed to protect the colonists, can adopt the physical form of an opponent's deepest fear and then use it to kill them. The colony is massacred and as retaliation the orbiting human navy nuke the planet. In revenge, the Spooks invade Earth.

In a last-minute attempt to avert the war, Seethan Bodell, a marine combat pilot sent home from the front with PTSD, is given a top-secret research spacecraft, and a mission to travel into the past along with his co-pilot and secret lover Rose, to prevent the original landing on Halloween and stop the war from ever happening. But the mission goes wrong, causing a tragedy later known as The Sundering, decimating the world and tearing reality, while Seethan's ship is flung into the future. The Spooks win the war and claim ownership of Earth. He wakes, alone, in his ejector seat with no sign of either Rose or his vessel. When he realises that his technology no longer works, his desperation to find Rose becomes all the more urgent – her android body won't survive long in this new Earth.

Gardens of Earth is the first book of *The Sundering Chronicles*. The story tackles alien war, a future that may be considered either dystopian or utopian, depending on who you ask, and a protagonist coping with his demons in an unfamiliar and stressful environment – not to mention immediate threats from a pathological serial killer, the remnants of Earth's inhabitants now living in a sparse pre-industrial society under the watchful eye of the Spooks, and returning human colonists intent on reclaiming Earth. Underlying all this are issues of social justice, human and android rights, and love that transcends difference. In many senses this is classic science fiction, but the abilities of the Spooks provide an environment, and archetypal creatures within it, that are reminiscent of myth and magic fantasy. Truly cross-genre, *Gardens of Earth* is an exciting adventure, a heart-rending quest, and an eye-opening insight into the coping strategies of a veteran.

ISBN: 9781911409953 (epub, kindle) / 9781911409854 (264pp paperback)

Visit bit.ly/GardensOfEarth

You might also enjoy

ENTANGLEMENT
DOUGLAS THOMPSON

FINALLY, TRAVEL TO THE STARS IS HERE

In 2180, travel to neighbouring star systems has been mastered thanks to quantum teleportation using the 'entanglement' of sub-atomic matter; astronauts on earth can be duplicated on a remote world once the dupliport chamber has arrived there. In this way a variety of worlds can be explored, but what humanity discovers is both surprising and disturbing, enlightening and shocking. Each alternative to mankind that the astronauts find, sheds light on human shortcomings and potential while offering fresh perspectives of life on Earth. Meanwhile, at home, the lives of the astronauts and those in charge of the missions will never be the same again.

Best described as philosophical science fiction, *Entanglement* explores our assumptions about such constants as death, birth, sex and conflict, as the characters in the story explore distant worlds and the intelligent life that lives there. It is simultaneously a novel and a series of short stories: multiple worlds, each explored in a separate chapter, a separate story; every one another step on mankind's journey outwards to the stars and inwards to our own psyche. Yet the whole is much greater than the sum of the parts; the synergy of the episodes results in an overarching story arc that ultimately tells us more about ourselves than about the rest of the universe.

Douglas Thompson's short stories have appeared in a wide range of magazines and anthologies. He won the Grolsch/Herald Question of Style Award in 1989 and second prize in the Neil Gunn Writing Competition in 2007. His first book, *Ultrameta*, published in 2009, was nominated for the Edge Hill Prize, and shortlisted for the BFS Best Newcomer Award. *Entanglement* is his fifth novel.

ISBN: 9781908168153 (epub, kindle) / 9781908168054 (336pp paperback)

Visit bit.ly/EntanglementBook

UNDERSIDE

Space opera meets gangland thriller

ZOË SUMRA

BOOK 1

SAILOR TO A SIREN

"If you like your space opera fast and violent, this book is for you"
– Jaine Fenn

When Connor and Logan Cardwain, a gangster's lieutenants, steal a shipment of high-grade narcotics on the orders of their boss, Connor dreams of diverting the profits and setting up in business for himself. His plans encounter a hurdle in the form of Éloise Falavière, Logan's former girlfriend, who has been hired by an interplanetary police force's vice squad.

Logan wants a family; Éloise wants to stop the drugs shipment from being sent to her home planet; Connor wants to gain independence without angering his boss. All of their plans are derailed, though, when they discover that the shipment was hiding a much deadlier secret – the prototype of a tiny superweapon powerful enough to destabilise galactic peace.

Crime lords, corrupt officials and interstellar magicians soon begin pursuing them, and Connor, Logan and Éloise realise they have to identify and confront the superweapon's smuggler in order to survive. But, when one by one their friends begin to betray them, their self-imposed mission transforms from difficult to near-impossible.

ISBN: 9781908168771 (epub, kindle) / 9781908168672 (288pp paperback)

BOOK 2

THE WAGES OF SIN

One young woman dies and another vanishes on the same chilly spring night. Connor Cardwain sees no reason to link his cleaner Merissa's murder to a mystery anchored within a high-end warship sales team, but reconsiders his position when he realises both women were connected to a foreign runaway.

Armed with an enterprising widow, an imperial spy and his own wits, Connor sets out to find the missing woman, in a city streaked with vice and a planet upturned by other ganglanders' ambition. If he fails to beat arms dealers, aristocrats, pirates and human traffickers at their own game, he and all his team will pay the price – and the wages of sin are death.

ISBN: 9781911409052 (epub, kindle) / 9781911409151 (312pp paperback)

Visit bit.ly/Underside

About Terry Grimwood

Suffolk born and proud of it, Terry Grimwood is the author of a handful of novels and novellas, including *Deadside Revolution*, the science fiction-flavoured political thriller *Bloody War* and *Joe* which was inspired by true events. His short stories have appeared in numerous magazines and anthologies and have been gathered into three collections, *The Exaggerated Man*, *There Is A Way To Live Forever* and *Affairs of a Cardio-Vascular Nature*. Terry has also written and Directed three plays as well as co-written engineering textbooks for Pearson Educational Press. He plays the harmonica and with a little persuasion (not much persuasion, actually) will growl a song into a microphone. By day he teaches electrical installation at a further education college. He is married to Debra, the love of his life.